up with the sun

T.D. COLBERT

For my babies. My world revolves around you.

UP WITH THE SUN

Book Two, Night & Day Duet

Copyright © 2023 T.D. Colbert

Published: T.D. Colbert 2023

Editing: Jenn Lockwood Editing

Cover Design: T.D. Colbert

www.tdcolbert.com

CHAPTER ONE

stevie

"HOW'S IT LOOK?" Della asks through the phone as I stare up at the tiny cottage in front of me. I drove ten hours to get to it, so honestly, it could be a trash can and I'd be kissing the ground in front of it. I'm just so damn happy to put the car in park and to know that I'm staying in the same place for a while.

"It's got a door and windows, and there's no one else around, so I'd say it's pretty perfect," I tell her.

She smiles.

"It's still so weird to me that you're staying in your ex-husband's new fiancee's cottage," she says, and I hear her chomp down on a carrot on the other end of the line.

"First of all," I say, reaching into the back of my car and yanking my suitcase out, "it's not hers. It's her aunt's." I slide out of the car and pull it out onto the ground. I reach back over the center console and grab my purse and a few other things from the passenger seat. "And second of all, we're not doing that. We're not talking about what's weird or fucked up about me being here. They're not here. They have nothing to do with it. It's a free place to stay, and the best part is that it is ten hours away from anyone and everything I know."

"Hey," Della says, feigning offense. I roll my eyes.

"Except for you, ya whore," I say. She giggles.

"Okay, you're right. Positive thoughts. I really am excited for you, Steve," she says. "You need this."

I sigh as I close my car door and look up at the cottage again.

"I do," I say. "I'm gonna go get settled. I'll call you later."

"Okay, love you," Della says.

"Love you," I say, then hang up. I take in a deep breath and walk toward the house, my suitcase dragging through the gravel behind me. It's a little house, but it's all I need. Except, when I get to the side of the house, my jaw drops when I see water. It's a deep, dark blue, and it's completely breathtaking. It's late September, so the air has a chill to it, sharper than home in Maryland. But I forget all about the chilliness when I see the bay. The water moves with the wind, crashing into the shore and the rocks that poke out from all sides of it. A few other small houses and cottages poke out from the trees and rocks across the water. But otherwise, it's just the sun, the sky, the water, and me.

And it's so beautiful that it makes the breath catch in my throat. I haven't seen something like this in a long time. I haven't *felt* something like this in a while.

Something that makes me feel lucky to be alive. To be a witness.

I smile.

Something else I haven't done in a while.

I turn back toward the door and pull the key out of my pocket. I unlock the door and step inside, and the first thing I notice is how cold it is.

I remember Marie's instructions: *there's a heater in the storage room to the right when you walk in. Turn that on right away. Then, light a fire as soon as you can. That will warm up the whole house. There will be logs in the basket by the fireplace, and more are stacked outside.*

I drop my things and immediately locate the heater, flicking it on. It makes a grumbly noise, shakes for a bit, then seems to turn on. Either that, or it's about to blow up. One or the other. Then, I walk toward the fireplace and throw a few of the logs on and look around for a lighter. I see one resting on a shelf next to the lamp in the corner of the room, and I flick it on, lighting the logs at different ends until they seem to catch well. Then, I roll back on my ass and sit right on the floor, staring into the orange flames as they grow. The whole cottage already smells like the fire, and I push back and lie against the green plaid couch that sits across from it. I look around slowly. In this room, there's just the couch, a loveseat, and a smaller rocking chair. There's no TV, just the fireplace. I see the stairs to my right, and behind me, light floods in from the windows on the back wall. I push myself up onto my feet and look out at the water, my jaw dropping again. I walk through

3

the door to the screened-in porch and breathe in the salty bay air.

Cade would love this, I think. But then my throat restricts, and I can't swallow. My heart rate picks up, and I feel like I can't breathe.

I hate how much I think about him, but I do.

A lot.

My therapist says that I have to let myself feel whatever I feel about Cade and the divorce. But I hate letting him creep in like that. Innocent thoughts that crowd my mind.

But when you love someone the way I loved him, you don't stop thinking about them. Maybe it becomes sporadic, but they are always there. And one of the hardest parts of this divorce is having to face that— knowing that, no matter what, part of Cade Waters will always be branded on me.

But he's ten hours south, starting his life with his soulmate. The woman I invited into our lives. The woman I asked to take my place.

I sigh as my chest gets tight.

"I need a fucking drink," I say to myself as I turn back for the door.

Three hours later, I'm lying on the couch, staring back and forth between the fire and the second bottle of wine that I've now finished by myself. I had packed a few bottles, knowing that I might not be able to get to a liquor store my first day here, and I was right. I needed them. I found an old radio on the counter in the kitchen earlier, so the only sounds coming from the cottage are the crackling fire and me singing along to classic '80s music.

And then suddenly, I want to take a bath.

Just as "Nasty Girl" by Janet Jackson starts playing, I start doing a strip tease—for no one but my damn self. I pull the sweatshirt up over my head and swing it around. Then, I let my pants fall to the ground. I rip the t-shirt off as I start to sing and dance to the chorus, strutting up the steps toward the bathroom on the landing. I unclip my bra and let it fall to the floor so that I'm just left in my panties. But then the *really* good part comes on. So, I turn back around and start grinding on the banister, shaking my ass down to the ground and standing back up. I drop my head and flip it back up, and when I do, I'm face to face with the hottest fucking human I've ever laid eyes on.

And he's staring at me, lips parted, eyes wide.

While I'm butt. Ass. Naked.

"Oh, my fucking God," I cry out as he says, "Shit, I'm sorry," in the exact same moment. I jog up the stairs to the bathroom and snatch one of the towels from the linen closet, wrapping it around myself. Then, I peek around the door frame and see him. His back is turned to the steps, and he's looking out the window— or at least, he would be if he wasn't still covering his eyes with his hands. I take the opportunity to scope him out. He's tall—almost as tall as the door frame— with thick, brown locks. His blue flannel is rolled at the sleeves, and I can make out the veins on his arms that make my insides quiver. His beard is trimmed nicely, and his jeans hug his ass perfectly. And suddenly, I feel myself start to get hot.

I should be freaked out right now that there's a strange man inside the house with me, but all I want to do is stare at him. This is so not like me. This is so not Stevie. But I don't care.

"Who are you?" I ask. He jumps, but he doesn't turn around.

"I'm, uh...I'm Cash," he says. "I'm the groundskeeper for Marie. I keep up the cottage for her while she's away or while she doesn't have, uh, guests. Which I presume you are. Which I presume she forgot to tell me about."

I smile. He clears his throat but doesn't turn around.

"Well, Cash," I say, and I feel that wine-induced confidence kicking in. "I've had a very long day. Actually, I've had a very long year." I take one step down, letting the towel drop ever so slightly.

"I, uh...I'm sorry to hear that. Hopefully your trip to Blue Bay will help ease that a bit," he says, still facing away from me. Half of me wants to laugh at how sweet he's being. The other wants to scream at him to turn around and look at how absolutely devastatingly sexy I am.

"You know what else might help ease it?" I ask.

He clears his throat again. "What's that?" he asks.

"Hot, steamy, sticky sex with a complete stranger," I say. Sober Stevie would be mortified. She would be asking a million questions, like, if he is married, or if he is an axe murderer. Sober Stevie would be telling

6

Drunk Stevie how fucking ridiculous she is. But luckily, Sober Stevie isn't here at the moment.

I see his shoulders move slightly, his head turning to the side. But just before he says anything, my foot slips off the step I'm on, sending me cascading to the bottom.

"Jesus," he says, spinning around and lunging for me. He grabs my arms and pulls gently. "Are you alright?" he asks.

I smile as he tugs the towel up from under my ass and helps me cover back up.

"I won't feel it till the morning," I say. "So, what do you say?"

He looks down at me, his face serious for a moment, then smiles. He stands up and holds out a hand to me.

"That sounds great," he says, "but how about a name first?"

CHAPTER TWO

cash

"THANKS, MICKEY," I say, giving him a smile and a salute as I slide the two coffees over the counter and leave a tip in the jar like I do every morning. I grab some sugar packets and a few creamers so she has all the options. Then, I walk back out onto Main Street and get in my truck that's parallel parked outside of Mickey's Cafe.

I put the coffees in my cup holders and set the bag of muffins down on my passenger seat before pulling off in the direction of Marie's house.

When I left last night, I made sure the strange woman staying in her house was fully taken care of.

Not in the way I wanted to, but the way I should have.

I exercised a *lot* of self-control. Especially with the way she was offering herself up on a platter.

I found out her name was Stevie. Which I fucking loved. Fleetwood Mac is my all-time favorite band. And I had—and still have—the biggest crush in the fucking world on Stevie Nicks. She had come up from Maryland, recently divorced, and her husband was now shacking up with some younger chick. Honestly, I was only half paying attention. I had helped her get upstairs and brought her suitcase up. I helped her get into a shirt before she collapsed on the bed. I brought her water and a few Advil from my truck and set them on the nightstand next to her.

And just as I was about to stand up from the side of the bed, she had grabbed onto my hand for a moment. Her eyes were still closed, but her grasp was strong. And even though I knew I couldn't stay, I really fucking wanted to.

I pull onto the gravel drive and park the truck behind her little black sedan. I grab the coffee and the muffins and walk toward the door. I go to open it, but I think twice. Technically, this is *her* place right now. So, I knock twice and wait. Through the window, I see her peek around the corner from the living room, then duck back in. She waits a beat, then comes around the corner. She's wearing a sweatshirt and sweatpants, and she looks fucking adorable.

She covers her face with one hand and opens the door with the other. Then, she lifts the other hand to cover the rest of it.

"Good morning," she mutters from behind her hands. "I cannot believe you came back here after the trainwreck of last night."

I chuckle as I hold up the coffee.

"We've all had those nights," I tell her as I close the door behind me. *I've had more than you know.* She just shakes her head as she spins around and walks toward the table.

She sits down and holds out a hand for me to do the same.

"Not all of us," she says, shaking her head again. I raise an eyebrow as I slide the coffee toward her. "I am usually, uh...much more controlled," she says. "And much more clothed."

Then, she covers her face again. I laugh as I slide over some sugar packets and the creamer.

"Hey, don't get me wrong," I say, holding my hands up. "I am a fan of no clothes. I just felt like maybe I should know who you were. And maybe, ya know, the first time shouldn't be when you were three sheets to the wind."

She smiles now, and my heart does this weird skip thing.

"I brought muffins, too. I don't think there's any food in the house."

She grabs the bag and digs through, pulling out a big, fat chocolate chip muffin.

"Thank you," she says. "You really didn't have to do this."

"Oh, I know," I tell her. "But I wanted to. Wanted to see what day two brought."

She smiles and shakes her head as she takes a bite. She opens one tub of creamer and dumps it in but leaves the sugar on the table. Cream, no sugar. Noted.

"So, you keep the house up for Marie?" she asks between sips and bites. I nod as I sip my own.

"I do. And about twenty other houses in the area," I tell her.

Her eyes widen.

"Whoa," she says. I shrug.

"It started with just some family friends that had vacation homes here," I explain. "But then, it grew. It's a decent side hustle."

She nods again.

"So, what's the main hustle, then?" she asks.

"I'm a bartender," I tell her with a shrug. Some women think it's cool. Some think it's a joke. Despite last night, she doesn't strike me as the laid-back, easily impressed type. I noticed the designer bags I carried to her room. But I won't be too quick to judge.

"Ya know, that's one industry that will never go out of business," she says. I smile and let out a breath of relief.

"So, how about you? We didn't get to go through much of the pleasantries last night," I say with a smile. She bites her lip and tucks a honey-blonde lock behind her ear. And while I watch it slip through her lips, I lick my own. I want a taste.

She clears her throat as she takes one more sip.

"I, uh…had a rough year," she says. I nod.

"You did mention that part, actually," I say.

"Shit, I'm sorry."

"It's fine." I smile. "I was a bit distracted. Go on."

"Well, anyway," she goes on, "I just, ya know, needed a change of scenery. I got a new job that lets me work remotely, and then I heard about this place."

"From Marie?" I ask. Her eyes flick to mine.

"From her niece, actually," she says. I nod.

"Oh, Tess? She's a sweet girl," I say. She clears her throat.

"She is. She's also the girl my husband is currently fucking."

I almost choke on my muffin. Not almost—actually. I *actually* choke on it. I start pounding my chest with my fist until my throat is cleared enough for me to inhale. She smirks and slides my coffee toward me.

"Easy," she says.

"I...uh," I say awkwardly, pausing as I take a too-long sip of my coffee. "I don't know how to respond to that. I had no idea."

She smiles and nods.

"You don't have to say anything. It's okay. I guess I shortchanged it a bit. They're not just fucking. They're sort of engaged. 'Soulmates' and all that shit."

My eyes are still wide. She's so matter of fact about it all.

"How...how did..." my voice trails off. I have so many questions, but I'm afraid to ask too much. I just met her, but I'm dying to know everything about her.

"How did they hook up? Uh, I sort of called her."

I just stare at her.

"You...you what?"

"They had a history together. He used to work with her dad. And he got his cancer diagnosis—" She pauses, and my eyes get wide again. "It's been a long year. You know how you can tell when someone just isn't all the way in it? They want to be, but maybe their heart isn't?"

I nod slowly.

"I do, actually," I tell her. I watch as her eyes widen a little bit. I want to hear more of this story. But as I stare at the beautiful woman before me, I can't imagine someone not choosing her. And I've known her for all of twelve hours. Maybe she's crazy? Has a lot of baggage? Or maybe the guy was just an idiot?

Stevie is one of those women that I imagine causing the slow-mo head turn in any room she walks into. The type of woman who just demands attention, simply by existing. And then, in the same breath, she's immune to it. She doesn't realize that the world is turned in her direction. Her blonde hair reaches her shoulders, and she has the front pinned back. Her eyes are this light, crystal blue, and she has tanned skin that makes them seem even brighter. Her lips are big and round, and everywhere else, she curves in all the right places.

"Sorry, enough about me," she says, shaking her head. "Anyway, long story short, I got divorced, and I wanted to be somewhere different."

I nod.

"Understood," I say. "But just so we're clear, I find you fascinating. I could listen to you all day."

She smiles, and her cheeks flush pink.

She's fucking beautiful.

"Well, why don't you tell me about you?" she asks. I suck in a sharp breath as I set my empty cup back down on the table.

There's so much weight in that question.

There's a lot to explain.

There's the stress of what to tell her and what to

leave out.

So, I just flash her my biggest smile and tap her hand.

"How about I give you a tour of Blue Bay first? You can ask whatever questions pop into your head on the way."

She looks at me and raises an eyebrow.

And then, I realize she doesn't know me. And I just asked her to get in my truck.

I pull my phone out of my pocket.

"Hang on," I tell her as I dial Marie. I let it ring, then I put it on speaker.

"Hello?" Marie answers.

"Hey, Marie," I say.

"How are you, Cash? Everything okay up there? Did Stevie get in okay?" she asks. I see Stevie smile.

"She sure did. Met her yesterday, actually. She seems great," I say, my mouth curling up into a half-smile. Stevie's cheeks flush again, and I want to kiss them.

"Oh, great. Thanks for always taking care of things up there," Marie says.

"My pleasure, ma'am," I tell her. "Was just letting you know she's in and settled."

"You're the best, Cash. Talk to you soon," Marie says, then hangs up.

I look up at her and shrug.

"That work for you?" I ask. "Now you know at least she trusts me." She smiles and stands up from the table.

"Let's go for that tour."

stevie

HE OPENS the door for me to get in his big red pickup truck, and as I settle in and put my seatbelt on, I smile. There's a cardboard sleeve for a coffee cup in one of the holders—and I noticed earlier that his was missing—but other than that, his truck is immaculate.

It looks like the inside of my car.

"You can tell you don't have kids," Della had said once when I was picking her up. She meant it as a compliment because my car was so clean. What she didn't know—and what I will never tell her—is how I cried in the bathroom once we got in the restaurant that night. About how I'd give anything to have baby puke and crushed Cheerios dirtying up my backseat if it meant that I had a child.

"So," I say once he gets in and puts his seatbelt on, "where to?"

He glances over at me and smiles. I'm pleased to realize this morning that he's just as attractive while I'm sober as he was when I was shitfaced. His square jaw twitches a little as he smiles, and I can't help but reciprocate it. His eyes are a deep, dark blue—just like the bay that we drive along on our way off the private drive where the cottage sits. They're fanned by long, thick lashes, and his beard is the same dark-chocolate color as his hair, sprinkled with some gray.

"Well, how touristy do you want to get?" he says.

I look at him and raise an eyebrow.

"I mean...I *am* a tourist, I guess," I say with a shrug. He nods.

"Okay. Then we'll go into town."

We drive for a few minutes, and I scan the little peninsula that we drive off of as we head more mainland. There are only a few other houses on the peninsula, and they are far apart.

As we get to the end of it, there are more houses. The bay narrows into a river as we cross a small bridge, and then, up ahead, I can see a little town. As we drive closer, I can't help but smile. If someone told you to picture a quintessential northern bay town, this is what they'd put on the postcard. Little shops line the main street. Couples and families walk in and out of shops, cups and ice cream cones in hand. Boats are docked at every corner. Seagulls are flying overhead.

And then, as we pull closer, like it's showing off, a mesmerizing lighthouse peeks out from across the water.

"That's Sherman's Point," he says, reading my mind as my eyes lock on it. "It's one of the oldest lighthouses in Maine. It's still in operation."

I nod.

"It's beautiful."

He smiles as he turns the truck into a spot on the street.

"It is. That's why the line to get in is out the door and wrapped around the whole freakin' bay."

I raise my eyebrows.

"I bet," I say. "It's still beautiful, though."

"It is," he agrees as he puts the truck into park. "But most of them are. They just aren't all front and center. Maybe I'll take you to see Glassy Point if you're up for it."

"Glassy Point?"

"My favorite lighthouse up here. If you wanna see it sometime, I'll take you."

My stomach flips. I've known this man for all of twelve hours, and for half of that, he only knew me as a drunken wine wench. But somehow, some way, he wants to make plans to see more of me.

"If I'm gonna be up here," I say, "I should probably know about all the good stuff, right? All the hidden treasures all the locals know about."

He smiles.

"Probably, yeah," he says. "You wanna walk around?"

I smile and nod, and we get out of the truck. He takes me into a few shops, we stop and get a hot pretzel at a place called Maude's, and then he takes me into one last souvenir shop. I look through all the little magnets and knick-knacks, and then I see him swipe something from a shelf and head to the register. He pays for it and takes the bag, smiling and nodding his head at the woman behind the counter. She smiles and fans her lashes at him, her cheeks flushing. I notice that about most women when we're near him. Like they can't help but look. Like their eyes are magnets. They gravitate toward him involuntarily.

He turns back in my direction and hands me the bag. I raise an eyebrow as I take it from him.

"Your first Blue Bay souvenir," he says. I open it and pull out a small glass bottle with a miniature ship inside. Painted on the side reads *Take Me Back to Blue Bay*.

I smile.

"I love it," I say. "Thank you."

He tips an imaginary hat.

"Shall we?" he says, motioning toward the door. He opens it for me, and we walk out onto the street. "How about some lunch?"

He leads me down a few more doors to a small restaurant that sits on the end of the street called Cooper's Tavern. A dock lines the side of it, with a few fishing boats tied up to posts.

"Hey, the man's here!" an old man calls from the back of the room as we walk up to the hostess stand. Cash smiles.

"Hey, Arch," he says with a wave.

"We haven't seen you yet this week. I was beginning to worry," the old man says.

"Never fear," Cash says. The old man looks around him at me and raises an eyebrow.

"Well, who do we have here?" he asks.

"Archie, this is Stevie. She's in town, staying at one

of the cottages I maintain. Figured I'd show her around."

I smile and stick out my hand.

"Well, it is nice to meet you, Miss Stevie," the old man says, his big bushy eyebrows covering his bright brown eyes as he smiles. "You all can just grab any table, and someone will be right over. Cash here will tell you all the best things to order. Although, he's been getting the same thing for the last three years."

"Hey," Cash says with a look and a devilish grin, "if it ain't broke, don't fix it."

"Nice to meet you," I say as Cash leads me through the dining room toward a door at the back. I follow him out onto a deck, and he holds his hand out to a small picnic table at the back corner that's right next to the water.

"Will this work?"

"Sure," I say. "This view is just *awful*," I joke as I sit down and put my purse on the seat next to me. He chuckles.

"This is Cooper's Inlet," he says. "It's usually packed, but you just missed the busy season."

I nod.

"It's beautiful," I say, looking around at the water, and the docks, and all the picturesque little store and restaurant fronts that poke out around us. Just as I'm painting a mental picture of him, his chocolate locks blowing in the breeze, his bronze skin glowing in the fading sunlight, a petite brunette with big brown eyes, round full lips, and the perfect size boobs appears next to us. She's definitely younger than I am—and defi-

19

nitely younger than him—and I almost cringe at the way smiles seem to appear on both of their faces at the exact same time.

Shit.

"Hey, you," she says with a smile as she pulls her pad out of her apron.

"Hey, you," he says back.

Ugh.

I swallow and wait to see how this plays out.

"Haven't seen you for a while," she says with a smile. "You hidin' from me?"

"Aww, never," he says, waving his hand. "Just been busy. Haven't been picking up as many shifts at the bar lately. Starting to winterize the houses."

She nods.

Co-workers. But judging by the way her jaw is tight, I'd say maybe something else has gone on here.

"Ah, yeah. That explains it. Winter'll be here before we know it." Finally, she turns to me, as if she is just now noticing that another person was at the table. She flashes me the same dazzling smile. "Hi, there."

"Hi," I say back, matching her grin. "I'm Stevie."

She nods and smiles again, looking from me to Cash, as if waiting for him to make some sort of introduction of his own. Figuring out where I come into the picture. But, unlike with Archie, he doesn't offer one. He just lets her sit awkwardly for a moment, then she raises her eyebrows slightly and puts a napkin down in front of each of us.

"Nice to meet you, Stevie," she says. "What can I get you guys to drink?" She shoots him a look.

I smile and look up at her.

"Can I get a Shirley Temple?" I ask. I know how juvenile it might sound, but it's my favorite drink. It reminds me of my teen years.

She smirks.

"Dirty?" she asks. I shake my head.

"Nope. Just a regular old Shirley, please." She nods and turns to Cash.

"Sure thing. And for you, whatever's on tap," she says assuredly. But he shakes his head, and her face drops.

"Actually, can I do a Shirley, too?" he asks, looking at me with a smile on his face that makes my heart race. "That sounds delicious."

"Um, okay," she says. "Be right back." Then, with a flip of her long brown locks, she turns and walks away.

"A friend?" I ask.

He smirks again, reaching back to anxiously rub the back of his head.

"Jamie? We work together at the bar sometimes. She's, uh…" His voice trails off. I chuckle and lean back in my seat.

"Don't worry," I say, holding my hands up, "I'm not the type to kiss and tell, either."

He smiles at me and nods, looking a little relieved.

Part of me wants to know just *how* complicated his relationship is with her. The other part of me has no interest in hearing about how another seemingly eligible man gets swept off his feet by a younger, tighter, trimmer model.

I've had enough of that for a lifetime.

"So, what should I order?" I ask him, desperate to change the subject. I pick up my menu, but he gently pushes it back to the table.

"No need for that," he says with a smile. "You're a Maine virgin. You're getting a lobster roll."

I laugh and nod.

"Deal."

Jamie comes back with our drinks, and he orders for both of us, which leaves her looking a little more displeased than the first time she walked away from our table. The sun is slowly going down, and there's a little hint of a chill in the air. I rub my arms, and instantaneously, he shimmies his jacket off and hands it across the table.

"You're definitely a Maine virgin," he laughs as he hands it to me. I go to put my hand up, but he shoots me a look. "It's only gonna get chillier. Take it."

I pull it on and immediately inhale him. There's this spicy, cedar scent to it that hits me right in the face and makes my stomach flip.

Jamie delivers our meals, and he waits patiently as I take a giant bite of mine, closing my eyes and humming with pleasure as I taste the freshest, most amazing lobster of my life.

"Well?"

I nod slowly.

"That's...amazing," I say. He smiles and takes a bite of his. Everything he does completely dazzles me. The way he chews. The way he licks his lips between bites. How his beard is trimmed and shaped so perfectly. The way his hands look worn and weathered but are also warm and soft. He's one of the most physically attractive men—no, just humans in general—that I've ever been in the presence of. But watching the way he talks to people, how he holds doors for everyone, how he smiles at strangers and friends alike. The way he's taken to me since I threw myself at him drunk and naked. *That's* what really makes my insides churn.

I'm starting to think he's just as attractive on the inside.

We finish up, and for the third time today, he pays the bill. Jamie gives us a sharp smile and nods as we stand to leave. It's almost completely dark now as he opens my truck door, then walks around to get in on his side.

"I should get you home," he says. "You've had a long day of being a tourist." I smile at him.

"I've gotta be close to local level at this point, right?" I say with a giggle. He shakes his head as he starts up the truck.

"No, ma'am," he says. "You still have a lot to learn." He pulls out of his spot as I turn to him.

"Well, thank you for taking my virginity," I say. His eyes dart from the road to me, back to the road. Then, we both bust out laughing. "To be clear," I say when I catch my breath, "I'm not a forty-year-old virgin."

He laughs again, and my body rattles.

"No, shit," he says. "Doesn't take a genius to see that."

My eyebrow shoots up.

"How do you mean?"

"Well, first of all, you're not forty yet," he says. I

swallow. "You told me that last night." I shake my head and smack myself in the forehead. "But even if you were, there is not a chance you are still a virgin."

I laugh again nervously.

"Why? Because I threw myself at you last night?" I giggle. "Oh, right. Because you know I was married."

He shakes his head again.

"Nah. Even if I didn't know all that," he says. I look at him again, curiously. I feel the air in the car get a little more serious as I swallow and tuck a piece of hair behind my ear.

"Then how?"

"Look at you, Stevie," he says, his voice lower now. "A man doesn't have to know you long to know that you will be one of the most beautiful people he'll ever meet in his whole life."

Before I can respond, he's pulling into the driveway of the cottage and putting the car in park.

"Wow," I whisper as I take off my seatbelt and turn to him. "That was quite a line."

He smiles and shakes his head.

"No line, Stevie," he says, his eyes on his hands. He slowly raises them to look at me,

and I feel this chill go down my spine. I don't know what to do. I know I need to get out, but I don't want to. I don't want the best day I've had in a very, *very* long time to be over.

"Well," I say as I reach for my handle, "this was perfect. Thank you."

He smiles and nods in my direction.

"You ready for part two?"

CHAPTER FOUR

I WATCH as she walks up the path toward the house. She's pretty perfect. Long and lean, her long blonde hair swaying behind her. She's a little older than most of the single women up here, but I find that really fucking attractive. It's not hard to tell that, at this point in her life, she knows what she wants and doesn't want. Not a lot of room for bullshit with her, which I appreciate.

But spending the whole day with her today has done nothing but make me want to spend more time with her. I know my time with her has a big ol' question mark stamped on it. She's just visiting from out of town. She's going through a lot of shit, and she doesn't need to add to it. She doesn't need *me* to add to it. But the fact that she works from here, that everything seems so open-ended, gives me this sense of hope and excitement. I could have another day, a week, a year. I have no idea. So, I don't want to let any of it go to waste.

We made plans for this weekend. She says she actually has to get some work in while she's here, and she starts virtually at the new job tomorrow. I pretend like waiting a few days to see her again is no big deal. But honestly, as I watch the cottage door close behind her, I'm hit with this unexpected sadness.

I haven't felt this light in a very, *very* long time. I came to Blue Bay so I could live a life of silence. Repent for all the shit I did back in the day. Stop myself from wreaking havoc on anyone else's life. Maybe find what I was looking for.

But then, she walked in like a fucking ray of sunshine just twenty-four hours ago, and there is a shift in my atmosphere.

Speaking of wreaking havoc, just as I'm pulling out of her driveway, my phone vibrates in my pocket. I reach down and pull it out, watching as my mom's name glows on the screen. I suck my teeth as I contemplate whether or not I should get my weekly phone call over with now. Luckily for her, Stevie has my spirits high, so I decide to give her a chance.

"Hey," I answer.

"'Hey,'" she mocks me, her familiar raspy voice coming through the phone. I can practically smell the cigarette smoke through it. "What a way to answer your mother."

I roll my eyes.

"What's up? How's it going?" I ask. I try to keep things light with my mom. Our relationship is tumultuous to say the least, and I've learned over the last few years—well, decades, really—that to keep my peace, I have to keep her at a distance. So much of the fucking turmoil in my life was caused by that woman. I won't blame her for the choices I made. Those are mine to bear. But I also won't ignore the fact that she was so strung out that she'd forget to leave me lunch money or pick me up from school. I won't forget that she didn't come to my high school graduation because her boyfriend of the week took her to Vegas.

I won't forget that, even as I became a man, she never took responsibility for who she was or what she did to me. That she's so stuck in her own ways, still such the victim in her own world, that she can't even begin to take responsibility for burning mine down. And I won't forget that she was too weak to pull me out of the hole she had dug for me.

"Ah, you know. Same shit, different week. Clay is sick," she says. I nod. Clay is her dead-beat "fiance"—although they've been "engaged" since I was twenty with no signs of actually making it official at any point in this lifetime.

"Sorry to hear that," I say. "How are you? How's work?"

She scoffs.

"I work at a drug store, Cash," she says. "How the fuck do you think work is?"

I clear my throat and tighten my grip on the steering wheel.

There's a long pause, and I hear her suck the smoke from her cigarette. I can picture her now, sitting on the same old, gray, tattered couch that's been in the living room for what feels like a fucking century.

"How's your little vacation up north going?" she asks. I roll my eyes again. I've been in Blue Bay for three years. But to her, it's a "vacation." Because God forbid I try and find some sort of happiness in my life rather than wallow in my misery as it seems I was genetically predisposed to do.

"It's great," I tell her every time she asks, even if it isn't always true. "Busier this time of year with all the winterizing."

"Uh-huh," she says, barely listening. "You know you're never gonna find her, right? That ship has sailed. It's time to get over it and move on. Stop dickin' around." I clench my fists, and I feel my jaw tighten as she speaks. *God, I hate her.* I hear the TV blaring in the background, and I know the conversation is coming to an end. At least, I hope it is.

She coughs and wheezes, and the sound sends me spiraling back through time—to the night I found her and her then-boyfriend overdosing in her bedroom, that same wheezing sound coming from her mouth as her eyes rolled back in her head. It was the first night I had to call 911 on my own mother. It was also the first time I tried heroin myself.

I feel my palms grow clammy, and I shake my head.

"Well, I'm almost home, and I have some things to do," I say, pulling into the driveway of the cabin I live in. "Good talking to you, Mom."

"Uh-huh, you too," she says, then hangs up before I can even say goodbye.

I walk up the front steps and unlock the door, dropping my coat on the entryway bench and kicking off my boots. I grab a beer from the fridge and walk to the big red chair that sits in front of the TV. But I don't turn it on. I just sit in silence for a little while, letting the memories of my mother fade away and reliving my day with Stevie in their place.

The next morning, I park my truck in front of Mickey's for my morning cup before I start the day. I have five houses to start prepping today, and the days are getting shorter around here.

But as I walk through the door, holding it for the elderly couple behind me, I stop in my tracks when I see her at the counter, smiling at Mickey as she takes her coffee. She freezes when she sees me, and that huge fucking smile that makes my dick twitch slides across her face.

"Morning. If I knew you hadn't already come in, I would have grabbed yours, too," she says.

I smile as Mick slides mine across the counter. I keep a weekly tab with him.

"No worries," I tell her, lifting my cup into the air. "And good morning to you."

"I, uh, realized this morning that I still have no food in the house. Guess I need to find a grocery store," she says with a laugh as she takes her coffee and the muffin she has in a bag and walks toward the door.

"Oh, yes," I say. "Food would be good. There's a

Henry's Grocery a few miles outside of town. That's the closest place."

There's a short pause, then I decide to shoot my shot.

"I could pick you up later and bring you, if you want?"

Much to my relief, she smiles again.

"Oh, that would be *great*," she says.

"What time are you done working today?" I ask.

She takes a sip of her coffee, then looks at me.

"I'll be done around five."

"Perfect. I'll be there then."

The day passes slowly despite that I haven't stopped moving since I left Mickey's. I'm finishing the last touches on my last house of the day, and finally, as I notice the sun sinking down over the water, I know it's time to pack it in and get headed in her direction. There's some pep in my step now as I pack up my tools and load them in the back of my truck. In fifteen minutes time, I'm pulling into the driveway of the cottage and practically hopping out of the truck before I even put it in park. I rap on the glass a few times, and she answers almost instantly.

"Hey," she says, pulling her purse strap up on her shoulder and pulling the door closed behind her. "Thank you so much for doing this."

I tip an imaginary hat.

"My pleasure, ma'am," I say. "Plus, I'm almost out of eggs." She smiles as I lead her to the truck, opening her door and closing it behind her. A few minutes later, we're pulling up to Henry's, and before I know it, I'm grocery shopping with Stevie.

Two days I've known her, and we're already grocery shopping together. I don't know why it feels like a big deal—it's not like we are going to be eating at the same house—but it does. I walk beside her as she adds things to the cart—mostly fruits and veggies, a lot of whole-grain shit, some eggs, coffee. I smile. It's not a mystery how she stays so, *ahem*, healthy. She eats like a professional athlete. She's walking in front of me a little ways now, and her tight little leggings sculpt perfectly around her ass. I'm practically drooling behind her when she turns to me.

"I think that should hold me for a while," she says. "Did you want to grab your eggs?"

I think about it for a moment, then smile and shake my head.

"Nah. If I need some, I'll just come steal yours," I say with a smirk. She nods and smiles back, and we head for the checkout. As we're loading the bags into my backseat, she puts her hand on her stomach.

"Man, I'm glad we just got food. I'm starving."

I think for a moment, then decide to shoot my shot again.

"I work at the bar tonight. We could go in a little early before my shift and grab some food if you don't feel like cooking."

She thinks for a moment, putting the last of the bags inside. Then, she looks up at me.

"Will your friend Jamie mind?" she says, a devilish

smile playing on her lips. The thought of her being possessive, a little jealous, maybe, over me? It makes my dick dance and tighten in my pants. I clear my throat.

"I won't know if she does," I say. "Because if you're there, there may as well not be anyone else in the room."

She looks at me for a minute, her lips twitching and dancing until she can't hold back the smile anymore. She bites her lip, trying to hide it, but she can't.

"What a *line*," she says again. "Fine. Dinner it is."

We take the groceries back to her place, and I wait while she changes into some jeans and a V-neck sweater that hugs her breasts perfectly. I've never been jealous of a sweater until this moment, but if I could be it, I would.

"Is it okay if we stop at my place real quick, just so I can change, too?" I ask her. She nods.

"'Course," she says. "Take me to the bachelor pad." Then, almost as quickly as the words come out of her mouth, she freezes. "Wait. It *is* a bachelor pad, right?"

My eyebrows knit together, and then it hits me.

She's asking if I'm single.

I look at her and smile as I start the truck.

"I haven't been in a relationship in over fifteen years, Stevie," I tell her with a chuckle. "It's a bachelor pad."

I see her breathe out a sigh of relief, and then we head off in the direction of my cabin.

It's a few miles inland, hidden up in the woods. I

got lucky. Mickey's cousin was putting it up for rent the week before I landed here in Blue Bay. I met Mickey at the coffee house while I was staying at one of the inns in town, told him I was looking for a place, and bam. I moved in about a week later, and I've been here since.

It's nothing fancy. His cousin had lived here before he got married, and his wife wanted more space. It was built for a bachelor, and that's how it's stayed. But it's got what I need. A bedroom, a kitchen, a couch to fall into at the end of a long day.

"Come on in," I tell her as I park in the driveway.

She gets out and closes her door, looking up at it.

"This is adorable," she says as she follows me up the steps. I pretend to cringe.

"Sexy, woodsy, manly," I tell her, joking. "Anything but 'adorable.'"

She laughs.

"Okay. This cute little cabin is super manly," she says. I put a hand on my chest and nod.

"Thank you, ma'am," I say as we walk inside. "Feel free to have a seat. Make yourself at home in my very masculine house. I'll be out in a sec."

I hear her laugh again as I walk into my bedroom and shut the door. I throw on a knit pullover, a clean pair of jeans, and my Timberlands. Before I walk back out, I spritz on some cologne, which I very rarely do. But for some reason, I want to make sure I smell good tonight.

We head off in the direction of Shanty's, the little

bar I've been working at since I first got here. It's on the very edge of town, right on the water. I take a breath as I prepare to let her in on a little more of my life.

Not too much of it, Cash. She deserves better.

CHAPTER FIVE

HE PARALLEL parks a little ways down from the bar, and we walk down the sidewalk to it. He holds the door open for me, then nods at the hostess as we walk in.

"You're here early," she says, her thick black curls held back in a headband. He nods and pats his belly.

"Man's gotta eat," he says. "Two, please." She looks at me, then looks at him and tries to hide a smirk as she grabs two menus.

"Right this way, *sir*," she says, leading us into the dining room.

She sits us down in a booth that happens to have a direct line of sight to the bar, and throughout our meal, his coworkers keep stopping by the table. He's definitely the big man on campus here, and there's no doubt they are trying to figure out who I am and what I am to him. It's funny to watch, and it's even funnier watching him let them fester, trying to figure it out. He introduces me only by name, which they all seem to linger on, like they're waiting for something more. But he never gives it to them.

About an hour later, he checks the time on his phone.

"I start in about a half-hour. I'll run you home quick," he says. I look around, though, and it's starting to get busier. More people file in, heading to the bar area, and I know that's where he's going to be. And suddenly, that's where I want to be, too.

"I have nothing to rush home for," I say with a shrug. "I can stay for a bit."

He looks at me and lifts an eyebrow.

"My shift doesn't end till one," he says. I smile.

"They have Ubers here in Blue Bay, right?" I ask. He looks at me like he wants to smile, but something is holding him back.

"Okay," he says, pulling some cash out of his wallet and throwing it on the table. Then, he slides his hand across the table and puts it on top of mine. I feel a tingle go through my body, down to my toes. "Stay. But if you do, you have to let me make you a drink."

I smile back at him.

"Deal."

I grab a seat at the bar right in the middle so I can be in the middle of the action—well, of *his* action— while he works.

"What do you drink?" he asks as he walks back behind the bar, making his way to me. I watch as several people reach across to shake his hand or fist-bump him. He really is popular here.

"Umm, usually wine," I tell him. "But I like whiskey, too."

He raises his eyebrows like he's surprised.

"A whiskey sour it is," he says, then turns away to make it. A few seconds later, he's back in front of me, putting it down on a napkin. He stands back and crosses his arms, waiting for me to try it. I lick my lips before bringing the glass to them, and I can't help but notice that his eyes never leave me. I put it back down, and he raises his eyebrows.

"Well?"

"You're pretty good," I tell him with a shrug. "I'll give it to ya." He smirks.

"I'll make sure to keep 'em coming," he says.

And he does. About an hour and a half later, I'm dangerously close to being drunk. Cash has been busy, sliding back and forth across the bar, taking orders, opening tabs, and delivering drinks. It's fun to watch him work. He's in his element, and the people love him —especially the ladies. And my insides burn a little every time one bats her eyelashes or sticks out her boobs in his direction.

But my attention is elsewhere when I feel a hand on my lower back and breath on my ears. I can smell the beer as he speaks.

"New here?" he asks. I turn to see a tall, dirty-blond man with a clean-shaven face, and a suit. He sticks out like a sore thumb in here, with everyone else dressed like they're going to their local bar and not to a work dinner.

"New-ish," I say. "And you?"

He smiles this weird, arrogant smile, like he pities me for even asking.

"My name's Kent Bilwither. You might have heard of Bilwither and Associates?" he asks, taking a sip of his beer. I just look at him blankly and shrug.

"I'm new in town," I say. He nods.

"Ah, yes, that explains it," he says. "If you're from this area, you know about Bilwither and Associates."

I look at him blankly again, waiting for him to elaborate on a subject I'm starting to care less and less about.

"It's the biggest real estate company in Maine. My father and uncle started it back in the eighties. Now, I help run it," he says, holding his beer out like he's waiting for me to faint or something.

"Sweet," I say, slowly turning back to my drink. But before I can completely spin the barstool around, I feel him grip my thigh, trying to turn me back to him. I grab onto the edge of the bar, trying to keep myself in place, but he yanks harder, his fingers digging into my leg.

I look around, and I feel my chest tighten. Cash is across the bar, talking to someone in the corner and making another drink. I shove his hand off of me and stand up.

"Don't touch me again," I say before I blow by him in the direction of the bathroom. I pull out my phone to pull up an Uber when I feel someone come up behind me.

"That was pretty rude," he growls in my ear, and I feel him press up against me, pushing me into the wall, my phone fumbling out of my hand onto the floor. I feel my breath quicken as I turn to face him.

He wouldn't possibly try something here, right? In this big bar full of people? But as I frantically look around, I realize there actually is no one around us right now. Just a long, empty hallway and loud music pouring from the bar yards away, drowning out anything else. My heart rate quickens.

"You need to step back," I tell him, trying to keep my cool. I feel the buzz making me unsteady, but I'm trying to fight it. I try moving by him in the direction of Cash and any other human, but he slams his arm against the wall, blocking my exit. "Step *back.*"

"I was just trying to talk," he says, bending his head down toward me. "That's all. And you dismissed me."

I look up at him, our eyes locking, and I narrow mine on his.

"I don't owe you conversation. *Move.*"

Slam.

His other hand lands on the other side of me, making me jump.

"Having trouble hearing tonight, Kent?" I hear Cash say, and instantly, I feel safe. Like I can breathe—or at least, let him breathe for me. He walks toward us, but Kent doesn't move.

"We're just talking," Kent says. "Go on back to your bar now."

He's such a condescending asshole. I want to punch him in his stupid, frat-brother face. But he's currently still got his arms on either side of me, and I can't move.

"Drop your arms so I don't have to do it for you,"

Cash warns, moving closer to us until he's only about a foot away. I can smell his cologne.

They stand in a stalemate for a moment, eye to eye, and my heart is pounding. Finally, Kent lowers his arm, and I bust out of it, moving behind Cash and catching my breath. Kent walks by but pauses to stop in front of Cash. He tilts his beer and pours what's left of it on the floor in front of Cash's feet.

"Oops, guess you'll need to have someone clean that up," he says, then walks away. I sink back against the wall and cover my face with my hands. My head is spinning, but it's not from the booze. I feel Cash's hands on my arms as my body starts to shake.

"Hey, you okay?" he asks. I nod my head, but I know the expression on my face says otherwise.

"Yeah, I'm okay," I say, trying desperately not to think about what might have happened if Cash hadn't shown up when he did.

"I'm sorry," he says. "I saw him follow you back here and tried to get out from behind the bar as fast as I could."

I want to smile at the fact that he was keeping tabs on me, but my body won't let me right now. It's too busy reminding me that I'm safe.

"It's not your fault," I tell him. "I'm just gonna get an Uber and head home." I go to reach for my phone, but he bends down and picks it up off the floor, handing it to me.

"No, no," he says. "I'm gonna take you." My eyebrows knit together, and I look down at my phone. It's only eleven.

"You're still on the clock," I say. He shrugs.

"One of the other guys is here," he says. "He'll cover for me while I bring you back."

I should push back, tell him not to go out of his way for me. But the thing is, I don't want to. I want to be with him. I want the feeling I have right now. Secure. Safe.

I nod, and he puts his arm around me, leading me back down the hall and through the crowd. He walks me out to his truck, helps me inside, then climbs in.

The ride home is quiet, and his eyes are dead ahead on the road until we pull into the driveway. When he puts the car in park, he grips the steering wheel so tight that his knuckles turn white under the bright porch light.

"I'm sorry about that asshole, Stevie," he says through gritted teeth. I see the veins on his arms getting more pronounced, and I reach a hand up to them.

"Hey," I tell him, "it's fine. Nothing happened. It's not your fault."

He shakes his head and swipes a hand down his face.

"It could have. With him, anything's possible," he says, turning toward me. "Kent Bilwither beat up his girlfriend a few years back."

I gasp, my eyes wide.

"Broke the girl's jaw. Then, miraculously, she ups and moves out of town. Word was that she bought a big house in Vermont somewhere. Rumor is that his dad paid her off so she wouldn't press charges. He's not a good guy," he says. I swallow. "I don't like thinking about what might have…" His grip tightens again, and I break his fingers from the wheel and take his hand in mine.

"But it didn't. Because you were there," I say. He looks at me, then nods. He opens his car door and gets out, then comes around to mine, taking my hand.

We walk to the door, and I feel this swirl of butterflies in my stomach. He unlocks the door with his key and goes in before me, giving the cottage a quick sweep before I go in. He walks back toward me, and I can't feel my toes. I swallow and look up at him, taking a step closer so we're chest to chest.

I look up at him, and he stares down at me. I see his Adam's apple bob.

Kiss me.

He swallows again, reaching a finger up to brush a piece of hair from my face.

"You don't want me, Stevie," he whispers, resting his forehead against mine for the briefest moment. Then, he kisses it and walks out the door.

CHAPTER SIX

cash

I PULL BACK UP to the bar and put the truck in park, but I don't get out. My body needs to cool. I need a reset—from the adrenaline and fury coursing through my veins at seeing his fucking arms around her like that, the way she winced in his presence, the fear in her eyes... I see red again. I tighten my grip around my steering wheel, but I know I have to simmer down.

And then, to have to pull myself out of that cottage when I took her home. To look down at her and just want to fucking devour her, to kiss those perfect lips, to stroke her cheeks with my thumb, to run my fingers through her hair.

Don't fuck with her. You don't deserve it. And she deserves better.

I blow out a long breath.

I've hooked up with a handful of girls since I've been up here. Most of them a little younger than me. It's been a steady cycle, but nothing that has ever stuck —on either end. I'm just the town bartender-slash-handyman. The out-of-towner who sticks out. But after a while, that loses its charm. And people wonder why I'm forty and haven't settled down. Why I don't have anything steady.

They don't know why.

And they never will.

It's why I never went home. Because it's a lot easier to avoid the questions in a town of three hundred, rather than the revolving door of rumors and hounding that is my mother and everyone I grew up with on the outskirts of Boston.

I'm about to get lost in thought, sucked down into the dangerous and debilitating rabbit hole of my past, when someone knocks on my window, and I jump.

I roll it down and see Jamie standing there.

"Everything okay with your friend?" she asks.

I swallow.

Jamie was one of the said hookups.

One of the ones that cycled on and off again for a few months. She ended up getting a legitimate boyfriend for a few months, so we broke it off.

"Yeah. Fucking Bilwither," I grumble as I stare out through my windshield. She sucks her teeth and shakes her head.

"It's unfair that pieces of shit like him get to walk around scot-free when the people they fuck with will carry it forever."

I swallow, my eyes widening.

The people they fuck with will carry it forever.

"Hey, um, Nick says it's slowing down in there, and

he could take the tips. So, he said if you wanted to call it quits for the night, he's got it."

Thank God.

There are only a handful of things I want to do right now, and not one of them is going back into that bar.

I want to curl up in the dark. Be alone. Breathe it all out. Prepare to face the next day.

That's sort of how I've operated for the last twenty-plus years of my life.

Enjoying people's company, having a good time, but keeping enough distance so I never hurt anyone else.

I nod.

"That would be great. I'm sort of wiped."

"I'll let him know. See you next week," she says, tapping on my door before she turns back toward the bar.

I pull out of my spot and turn the truck around in the middle of the street, heading toward my house. And when I get to the fork in the road, where I go left for her cottage or right for mine, I idle for a minute. God, I want to go back so badly. Knock on the door, scoop her up, hold her close to me, kiss every inch of her.

But I'm fucking scared. Because this doesn't feel like one of those things that I could just walk away from. That *either* of us could walk away unscathed. So, I turn right, drive four miles, get to my cabin, and go to bed.

～

I wake up before first light, something I've been doing the last few years for no good reason. There's no real reason for me to be up this early. I don't have a job that requires it. I don't have kids running around or an animal to take care of.

It's just me and these woods.

I sit up and put my feet on the floor, running a hand through my hair. I walk across the hardwood toward my dresser and pull out a clean shirt. I pull it on, then a pair of gray sweats, and walk toward the closet. I reach up onto the shelf for a hoodie, but when I grab it, something falls off to the floor. And when I bend down to pick it up, I almost collapse.

The letter that she wrote me, when we were seventeen, right before everything. Before I took everything from both of us.

My hand shakes as I pick it up, still folded and tucked into a perfect square, the way she used to fold all of them. But there's a reason I kept this one for so long.

This is the one she wrote the day before it all happened.

When she felt me slipping through her fingers.

The note she wrote when she begged me to stay with her. To remember what we had, what I was, separate from the woman who raised me.

I can't open it. I can't look at it anymore. Instead, I just slip it back into the shoe box that I've kept it in all this time and leave it there until the next time it rocks my whole fucking world.

As I sit back down on my bed to put on my boots, I realize what a fucking sign it is.

The note. The reminder of everything I did, all that I took away.

Don't do it again, the universe is telling me. *Don't take it away for someone else.*

I throw myself back on my bed, one hand under my head, the other on my chest. And all I can see is Stevie's face.

How the fuck am I supposed to avoid something I can't seem to go an hour without thinking about?

stevie

I'M LYING in bed after snoozing my alarm for the third time, staring up at the wood-planked ceiling. I can hear waves crashing against the rocks outside my window, and if I wasn't so defeated from last night, I would probably feel pretty damn peaceful right now.

"You don't want me, Stevie," he had said. Like he knew, after two days, what I did and didn't want? Like he knew anything about me at all.

Ugh. But as I lie here, rerunning the conversation through my head, I realize just that. He *does* know a thing or two about me. It's been less than a week, and I've let myself be pretty damn vulnerable with him on more than one occasion. He knows why I'm here. He knows what I'm running from.

I thought I knew Cade, and then five years later, I was packing up the house we built together and ending the life I had known.

If I've learned anything over the last year, it's that time isn't the end all, be all. You could know someone for your entire life and still not really *know* them. And the more time I spend with Cash, I'm learning that the opposite might be true, too. Maybe you don't have to know someone for a certain amount of time before you know that you're safe with them. Or maybe, if you've been broken enough, you're not scared to break anymore. You're not scared of the letdown because you've learned to depend on yourself.

But for the second time since I met Cash...for the second time this *week*...I threw myself at him. I let him know that I was his for the taking, if he wanted me.

So much swirls through my head. Maybe he's gay? Maybe he really is into younger women? Maybe I'm not his type? But every excuse that pops into my head feels like it doesn't fit.

You don't want me. Like he was doing it for my benefit. Like he was walking away to protect me.

But from what?

Maybe I should heed his warning. Maybe I should take it to heart. Twice and no dice. Maybe I should let it lie. And as much as my brain knows this is the safest play, my heart is screaming at me not to listen. To take the plunge. To try again.

But my heart has misled me before. And I'm not giving that bitch another chance.

I moan and groan as my alarm goes off for the last time, one final warning that I need to walk downstairs and at least turn my computer on. It's been a week since I saw Cash last, and life here has been painfully quiet. I was spoiled my first few days here with insider experience, companionship, laughter—not to mention, getting to look at him.

But I guess I came on too strong. And I blew it.

It's probably for the best.

I have no idea how long I'm staying here. I have no idea about what my life will look like a week, a month, a year from now.

I'm just taking it one day at a time.

I'm surviving right now. But I will thrive again.

I just need time.

I pull a sports bra on over my head and pull up a pair of joggers. I don't have any meetings today, so this will be my attire—the joys of remote work. I pull my hair up into a bun. I chopped it when Cade and I first split, and I've let it grow out now a little past my shoulders. It's still shorter than I've ever worn it, but there was something cathartic about cutting it. Like I was helping speed up the process of regenerating myself into a version he had never touched.

I'm enjoying the new job. I can tell I'm going to have a lot of creative freedom while also not feeling so bogged down that I can't step away. But that's the problem...there's not a whole lot to step away *to*. Back home, I'd go to the yoga studio or meet up with Della and some of our other friends for drinks or dinner.

Here, it's just quiet.

Which, ironically, is what I thought I wanted.

But now that I'm really getting a taste of it, I'm not so sure.

Just as I look down at the time and realize it's half past noon and I haven't eaten anything, there's a knock on the door that makes me jump.

I see Cash standing on the other side of the glass, and I swallow. As I stand to answer it, I realize I'm still in just a sports bra. But he's seen all the goods. He's been offered them on a silver platter, and he said no. So, he can look all he wants to.

As I get closer to the door, he holds up a brown bag in one hand and a drink tray with two cups in it in the other.

I open it, and he smiles.

"Thought maybe you could use a lunch break," he says.

I raise an eyebrow at him but open the door wider. As he walks by, I see his eyes trail my body, and I bite my lip to keep from smiling.

That's right, sir. Take a good, hard look.

He sets everything on the counter and starts going through the bag. He pulls out two burgers, two fries, and some napkins.

I just stand there, arms crossed, watching him. He turns to me as he slides one meal over in my direction, and our eyes meet.

"Not hungry?" he asks, looking deflated.

"Hungry, yes," I say. "Confused...also yes."

He clears his throat and leans back against the counter. His arms bulge out of his t-shirt, and it's all I can do not to just fucking stare at him. He's just *so* damn pretty. He sighs and rubs the back of his head.

"Look, Stevie," he says, "I'm sorry about last week. I…"

"You don't owe me an apology," I say, holding up my hand and walking toward the counter to grab one of the burgers. But he puts his hand on mine and stops me.

"Stevie, I need to say this, okay?" I freeze, and our eyes lock. God, he really is gorgeous. "Last week, I left not because I didn't want to take you up on your offer. I left because I *wanted* to take you up on it. I wanted it *too* much." I raise an eyebrow. He smirks, and his eyes drop. He shakes his head gently, like he's trying to find the words. Then, he steps toward me so that our chests are almost touching, and he looks down at me from his long, fanned lashes. "You are the most beautiful woman I've ever met, Stevie. And I don't even know your fucking last name." He chuckles as he says it. "I'm not jumping your bones the second I meet you like some kind of animal. You deserve better than that."

Then, he steps back slowly. I think for a minute, then I take a step closer to him.

"First of all, you hardly know me. You don't know what I do and don't deserve. Second of all, it's Rhodes. And third," I say, reaching around him to grab the burger, "I'm almost forty years old. I think I can handle a hit-and-quit by now, if that's what it is. But hey, I'm grown. If you're not interested, I know my way around. I can take care of things myself."

And then, I smile and scoot around him, walking out the back door and sitting on the porch. A moment later, he follows through the screen door and sits on the chair next to me, unwrapping his burger and looking up at me.

I smile as I take a bite.

"What?" I ask, licking ketchup from the corner of my mouth.

He shakes his head.

"That might be one of the hottest things a girl has ever said to me," he says, "and at the same time, it was a kick to my pride."

I laugh and shrug as I chew.

"It is what it is," I say. "But hey, thanks for lunch."

He smiles and nods.

"My pleasure. How much more work do you have today?"

I look down at my phone.

"Well, it's only one," I say. But he just looks at me, eyebrows raised, as if to say, *and?* I laugh. God, it feels good to laugh. "I can probably tie things up in the next twenty minutes or so. Why?"

He leans across and grabs the empty wrapper from my lap, crumpling it up in his hands as he does the same with his own.

"Make it fifteen. We're going on our next adventure," he says. Then, he walks back into the house. I smile and shake my head, even though I know that in fifteen minutes, I'm going to be walking out that door with him.

I throw on a sweatshirt and lace up my sneakers, putting on a few strokes of mascara before I walk back down the stairs. He's waiting in the kitchen, kneeling down by the wood-burning stove, fiddling with something. He stands when he sees me.

"I need to fix this when we get back," he says.

"What's wrong with it?" I ask.

"I think a few of the bolts are just loose. Might need to be oiled, too. Just a quick tune-up."

I nod as if I know what any of that meant, and then he opens the door and lets me walk out first. He locks the door behind us, and there's something that feels so strangely comfortable about us both having a key to the same house.

We get in his truck, and he starts it up, looking over at me. It's extra chilly out today, and this sweatshirt isn't cutting it. He smiles, then reaches into his backseat and pulls a large flannel jacket into the front. He lays it on my lap.

"You're gonna need this," he says. "Fall hits different up here." I want to say no, that I'll be fine, but once I get a whiff of it—of him—I know I'm wrapping myself in this thing for the rest of the damn day. He pulls out of the driveway and down the lane until we reach the main road and start heading in the opposite direction of town.

"You gonna tell me where we're going?" I ask him. He smiles.

"One of Blue Bay's best kept secrets," he says. "And my absolute favorite place." I look at him with wide eyes, waiting for the big reveal. He laughs. "We're going to a lighthouse."

"Oh!" I say, clapping my hands together excitedly.

"A lighthouse! Is it the one we saw at lunch last week? The one with the bridge?"

He shakes his head.

"Nope," he says with a smile. "But I promise it's worth it."

About twenty minutes later, we're pulling onto another gravel road lined with a white fence and big, tall oak trees on either side. They're so big that they form a tunnel, and I can't see what's through them at the end. We drive for almost a mile before we finally reach the end of the lane, and he pulls off to the right and parks the truck. And in front of us, sits the most adorable, quaint, perfect little lighthouse I've ever seen. We get out, and I stare at it in awe. There are no other cars in the lots, and I look around.

"Are we...allowed to be here?" I ask. He chuckles.

"I know a guy," he says with a shrug. "Come on."

We walk past a wooden sign that reads, *Glassy Point Lighthouse, Est. 1792.*

"Wow," I whisper, and he turns and looks at me.

"It's one of the oldest lighthouses in Maine," he says, "and one of the few in this area still in use."

My eyes widen as we walk toward it.

"It's still in use?" I ask. He nods.

"A friend of mine is the keeper," he says. "Chuck. It's only open to the public a few days a week. Today is not one of those days. So, that's why we're here." He pauses for a minute as he watches me walk up to it. I put my hand against the white bricks, looking up at it. It's not the most beautiful lighthouse I've ever seen, but there's something pretty magical about being the only two people here right now. About getting to see its beauty when no one else does. About standing next to this thing, this beacon of hope, this saving grace to passing ships. I jump when I feel his breath on my cheek from behind.

"Wait till you see it from the other side," he whispers. Our eyes meet for a brief moment, then he moves around me and juts his head in the direction he wants us to walk. I smile and pull his flannel around me tighter as I follow him. And as we walk around the lighthouse, my jaw drops when I see the water—endless, deep, blue water as far as my eyes can see, only stopping when it meets the sky. A cliff drops below us, and suddenly, it's just us, the trees, the water, the rocks, and this lighthouse.

"Okay, now turn around," he says. We do, and then, I see exactly what he means. It's not grand. It wasn't built to be jaw dropping. It was built to be a saving grace. The last ray of hope. And that's what it is right now.

"This is...perfect," I whisper. He nods as he steps up closer to me, our shoulders touching now.

"Yeah," he says. "I stumbled on this place when I first moved up here a few years ago. I met Chuck, and he gave me the rundown. I like it because it doesn't get all the glamor like some of the other ones do. But it's just as important."

I look at him, and our eyes meet. He smiles and shakes his head. "Kinda corny, huh?" he says. I smile back at him.

"Yeah," I say. "But it's also pretty beautiful. Thank

you for bringing me here. Thanks for sharing your place with me."

He smiles down at me.

"I know, as you pointed out earlier, I 'barely know you,' but you strike me as someone who could use a place. So, you can share mine when you need it. You have my permission."

I smile. I *could* use a place.

"Well, thank you, sir," I say. "That means a lot."

"So," he says, taking a few steps toward the house and pulling his keys out of his pocket, "you wanna see the inside?"

My eyes widen as I look at him.

"You have a *key?*" I ask him in disbelief.

He nods.

"I told you. I know a guy," he says with a wink. "Come on."

I do a little jog to catch up to him, and we walk around to a door on the side of it. He unlocks it and opens it, and I walk inside. It's musty, pretty much exactly what you'd think a one-hundred-fifty-plus-year-old lighthouse would smell like on the inside. It's dark, but there are a few windows that let in enough light to see. He takes my hand, and I don't even think about it until he's leading me up the spiral staircase, how natural it feels having my hand in his. How natural all of this feels. Just following him, letting him drive me around, letting someone take the reins and just let me take it in.

I've known him for less than two weeks, but it feels so different. It feels foreign, but *he* doesn't. The comfort

I feel, the quickness with which we became friends, how fast I felt like I could air out my dirty laundry. It's a big oxymoron with him. It feels foreign, but it feels familiar. It feels fast, but it feels like I've known him forever. And the time I spend with him, I lose track of completely.

We get to the top of the staircase, and he waits for me at the top. Then, he walks me over across a creaky wood floor to the light in the middle of the tower. It's beautiful.

I mean, in reality, it's not. It's old and looks like parts—or all of it—should have been replaced a long time ago. But it's perfect. There's a small, antiquated desk in the corner of the room with some things written down. Against another wall sits a bed on an old metal frame.

I look at him.

"I told you, it's still in use. When the weather's bad, Chuck stays here," he explains. I nod. "Now, come with me for the best part," he says, sticking his hand out to me. I take it, and he leads me across the floor to the big window that the light points to. He opens a latch and climbs out, standing on the balcony outside of it. Then, he reaches back for my hand. I swallow. If there was ever a time to let him know I was afraid of heights, this would probably be it. But he just looks so damn pretty, the sun making his tan skin glow, his hair blowing in the breeze, those blue eyes matching the water behind him. I take it, and he pulls me out with seemingly no effort. I cling to him as I catch my balance, and we scoot along the narrow balcony a little ways until we're right in the center of it. Then, he sits down slowly, letting his legs dangle off. He pats the spot next to him. I swallow, then lower myself slowly. I let out a shaky breath as I sit down, gripping tight to a pole of the railing.

"You okay?" he asks. I blow out a sharp breath and nod, forcing a smile.

"Just get a little shaky high up," I say. He nods.

"Shit, I'm sorry. Wanna go?" he asks.

But I shake my head.

"No, no, just…give me a minute," I say. He nods again. Then, I feel him scoot a little closer to me. He puts his hand on top of my free one and wraps his fingers around it.

"Try looking out," he says. I look up at him, and he nods his head in the direction of the water. I slowly turn my head and let out another sharp breath. "Look at the trees. Look how they line the inlet. See that out there? Way out there, around that bend? That's Sharpton Point." I look out toward where he's pointing. I follow his finger as he points out where certain things are along the coastline, and when he looks back at me and smiles as he talks, my stomach flips. And suddenly, I don't feel so afraid of the height anymore. He leans into me. "Feelin' better?"

I nod.

"Little bit, yeah." I smile back. A gust of wind blows, and I quickly tighten my grip on the pole. He smiles as he scoots closer, pushing a stray piece of hair out of my face.

"Good," he says, his voice just above a whisper. I

look at him, our eyes locked. I want to know everything about him. I want to know his fears, his happiness. His story.

"Tell me something," I say. He cocks an eyebrow.

"Like what?" he asks.

"Anything. Just tell me something about you."

He smiles and leans his head back a little, drawing in a long breath.

"Hmm," he says, looking out over the water. Then, he looks back at me. "The three years I've been here in Blue Bay have been some of the most peaceful of my life."

I look at him, my eyes wide.

"Why here? What brought you here?" I ask. He shrugs.

"Just an opportunity," he says. "A guy I knew from work had a house up here. Mentioned he needed to find a groundskeeper. I took him up on it. And then, when I got here, I got the job at the bar, met more people, and got more houses to keep."

I want to ask for more, but he just looks so beautiful in this moment that I decide to sit in it for a minute. Then, he stands and reaches a hand down for me.

"We done here?" I ask him, trying not to sound as disappointed as I feel. He smiles as he pulls me to my feet.

"Almost," he says. And then, without any warning, he slides a hand around my waist and pulls me closer to him. His other hand slides across my cheek, and he grips the back of my head, his fingers in my hair and his thumb stroking my jawline. "Before we go, we're gonna have our first kiss right here."

Then, he pulls me in closer and bends down till his lips crash into mine. It's soft at first, then a little more intense. I slide my hands up his arms, one draped over his shoulder, the other clasping the back of his head. My fingers and toes start to tingle as I press my body against his, and my stomach flips over itself over and over again. I feel my whole body go limp in his arms, but I'm still standing in his grip. When we finally come apart, we stand for a moment here on this balcony, our foreheads pressed together. I clear my throat as he creates a little more space between us, looking down at me to see where my head is at.

"Well?" he asks with a smirk.

"Not bad," I say, feeling my cheeks flush. "It's interesting that you called it our 'first' kiss. That insinuates that you think there will be more."

He smirks again, leaning into me.

"I think after *that*, it's safe to assume we will be having *many* more kisses."

CHAPTER EIGHT

cash

WE'RE RIDING BACK into town, and I'm reeling from the kiss. All I want to do is pull over and do it more. I was two seconds away from whisking her off that balcony and taking her to the bed in the house. But who knows how long it's been since Chuck changed the sheets. I pull the truck into the big lot at the edge of town and park. We get out and start walking, and I want to hold her hand so fucking bad. I want to let her know that here, in this little world, I want her to be mine. I know what I'm doing. I'm compartmentalizing. My heart is saying that our world here in Blue Bay is safe. That the rules don't apply here.

That the hurt I've caused won't follow us here. And it won't follow her out of it, if she ever leaves.

God, that's something I never want to fucking think about.

I know I'm wrong. I know all of it is complete bullshit. But for right now, I'm going to let that part of me win.

We walk around downtown for a bit, in and out of more shops. I introduce her to a few of the small business owners that I've come to know over the years. And then, I drag her into another souvenir shop. I whiz by her toward the counter, I say hi to Mel while she's perusing the t-shirts, and I quickly point out the bracelet I've had in mind since we got to town today. It's been in this case for over a year, and it's always caught my eye. I just never had anyone to buy it for. Until now. I shove the cash over the counter and tell her to keep the change, and she hands it to me, motioning for a box. I wave my hand, and she hands it over quickly, just in time for Stevie to round the corner.

"Get anything good?" she asks just as I'm safely stuffing it in my pocket. It will be hers—just at the right time.

"Oh, I was just catching up with Mel here," I say, nodding to Melanie. She picks up what I'm putting down and quickly jumps in. She smiles at Stevie and sticks her hand out from across the counter.

"Hi there," she says, "I'm Melanie."

"Stevie," she replies, "it's nice to meet you."

"You visiting?" Melanie asks. Stevie looks at me, then back to Melanie and nods.

"I am. Staying in a rental cottage a few miles outside of town," she tells her. Melanie nods.

"And how do you know Cash?" she asks, her eyes darting from Stevie to me, back to Stevie. She bites her lip to find a little smirk. All women should be some sort of FBI agent. They can always find out the information they're looking for.

"He keeps up the house I'm staying in, actually," she says. Her cheeks flush, and I know it's because she's thinking of the night we *actually* met. We both are. "He's been kind enough to show me around town."

And make out with you about fifteen minutes ago.

"Ah, well, that Cash sure is a gentleman, isn't he?" Melanie says with a playful smile. She's tiny, about five feet tall, with curly red hair and big green eyes. She and her husband, Sean, own the shop and a gas station a few miles outside of town.

"So far," Stevie says with a playful smile, and Melanie laughs.

"Well, let me get this girl some food," I say, leading her back out of the shop. "See you soon, Mel. Tell Sean hi."

"Will do. Nice to meet you!"

Stevie waves back as we exit the doors and turn toward one of my favorite little restaurants on the water that's a few doors down.

"Everyone talks about southern hospitality, but everyone up here so far has been so freakin' nice and smiles like a Stepford wife," she says. I laugh at her joke, and instinctively, my hand finds hers. We both pause for a minute as she looks down at them together. Then, our eyes meet, and my heart starts to race. But to my relief, she smiles and interlocks our fingers, and we keep walking like it's perfectly natural.

I lead her into Smokey's, and we get seated pretty quickly at a booth in the corner. But just as we're about to sit down, I hear my name being roared from the other side of the room. It's Nick, and in tow are Jess, Cammi, and Jamie. Nick gives me a hug, and so do all the girls, like we don't all see each other four times a week at the bar. But they've become my family in a way. I'm happy to see them, but this isn't exactly how I envisioned the rest of the evening going. Selfishly, I wanted to have her to myself. I wanted to keep going down that spiral of my world slowly becoming just me and her, right here, right now.

Maybe this is some sort of divine intervention.

"Hey, guys," I say as I greet each of them. Then, I turn to Stevie, who is smiling and waving to them. "I don't know if you guys got to officially meet the other night. But this is Stevie."

They all take turns saying hi to her.

"Sorry about that asshole the other night," Nick says with an eye roll. "He's such a fucking prick."

Stevie smiles, but I can see her skin flushing. She doesn't want to think about it, and she certainly doesn't want to talk about it.

"He won't be bothering her again," I say, sliding my hand up her back and turning back to them. They seem to all catch the drift, and then Jamie pipes up.

"We were just about to get a table over in the bar. You guys want to join?" she asks with an overly warm smile, like she's trying almost too hard to make it seem like this is totally normal. But to my surprise, Stevie smiles and nods.

"Sure, that would be great," she says, following them toward their table. She gives me a quick smile and eyebrow raise as she grazes by me. *God, I want to finish that kiss.*

We sit down at a high-top table, order a round of beers and bar food, and we all start talking and shooting the shit. Then, somehow, the subject gets back to me, and I feel myself grow a little tense.

"We didn't know what we were getting when this tall, dark, handsome stranger blessed Blue Bay with his presence a few years ago," Nick says with a toss of his head, and he starts to fan himself playfully. "But man, did he swoop in and make all the girls lose their minds."

I shake my head and take a swig of my beer while Jamie clears her throat uncomfortably. Stevie also takes a sip of her beer, and Nick quickly realizes how awkward he's made things.

"But seriously, though," he says, "this town needed him. Still don't know what brought you to Blue Bay, but glad you came, man."

Cammi looks over at me, her long black hair up in a messy bun on the tip-top of her head.

"Why *did* you come here?" she asks. "I don't think I've ever heard that story. You just showed up one day out of thin air."

I clear my throat and take another sip of my beer.
Fuck.
I came for a dream that turned out to be bullshit.
I shrug.

"I was just...looking for something different. And I found it here," I say, then my eyes drift back to Stevie. *I sure as hell did.*

66

We spend another hour or so there, laughing and talking about some of the crazy shit we've seen at the bar, the dumb questions people ask during the tourist season, how bad this winter is supposed to be. The girls ask Stevie some questions about where she's from back in Maryland, and I soak in every word.

It's a small town called Dalesville, about an hour outside of D.C.

She and her ex built a house there a few years back.

She doesn't get into all the gory details like she has with me, but I slide my hand down her thigh whenever she mentions him. I want her to know that I'm hearing her, that I feel for her, but also, that I'm claiming her. He no longer has permission to take space up in her mind or heart.

I might be the new guy, but up here, as far as I'm concerned, I'm *her* guy.

The DJ kicks on some music, and Cammi and Jess start moving toward the floor, waving at the rest of us to follow. Nick slams his empty bottle down on the table and takes Jamie's hand, leading her to the floor.

I look over to Stevie.

"Do you dance?" she asks me. I lick the beer from my lips.

"I'll do anything with you," I tell her, then I stand up and take her hand, leading her to the floor. We spin around, moving to the music, laughing and smiling. I feel her press her body up against me, and there's this heat that has nothing to do with the actual temperature. I feel myself get hard beneath my pants, and I want her to know. I want her to feel what she's doing to me. I take her hand and let her spin out, and just as I'm about to spin her back in and hold her against me, she freezes, her hand dropping from mine. She's staring, eye to eye, at another woman across the floor.

"Mom?" she asks, her eyes wide.

Well, that's a quick way to get rid of a boner.

She walks off the floor toward the woman, and I wait cautiously behind, moving closer at a snail's pace.

"What...how did you find me?" she asks, crossing her arms over herself. The second she saw her mother, her body language instantly changed. Like she was crawling back into her shell. Her mother is tall with blonde hair, like Stevie's, cut short. She's wearing black pants, a dressy blouse, and heels, and she has a big red purse that hangs from one shoulder. She's taller than Stevie, and she's staring down at her with this look of pure disappointment. Pure disdain, almost. Like she's disgusted with what she's seeing. And I feel all the hairs on the back of my neck stick up. I feel my hands clench.

"So, this is what you've been doing?" her mother says. "Playing around in some shithole bar, just drinking your life away without a care?"

Stevie tucks a piece of hair behind her ear.

"How did you find me?" she asks her again. Her mother scoffs and digs into her purse.

"Oh, please. There are like three people in this whole town. I asked around at a few spots. Not hard. There's nothing here."

I don't like how this is going. I don't like the tone

she's talking to her in. So, I step up next to Stevie, and I feel her side-eye me.

"Mom, this is Cash," she says, pointing to me. "He helps keep up the cottage I'm staying in. He's been showing me around town. Cash, this is my mom, Cindy."

Instinctively, I would normally stick my hand out for a shake. But I watch as she looks me up and down, from my boots to the top of my head, that same look of disgust in her eyes, and I decide to skip the pleasantries.

Instead, I give her a curt nod and settle next to Stevie, letting our skin touch so she knows I'm here.

I've got you.

"Ahh, now I get it. *This* is why you've been playing around," she says, waving her hand to me like I'm a piece of meat and not a person standing right here and perfectly capable of hearing her. "Living out a lumberjack fantasy and falling off the map while your life passes you by. Jesus Christ, Stevie. The holidays are coming up. Haven't you done enough fucking around? It's time to come home."

"Mom—"

Other people are starting to notice there's something going on, including the crew we've been with. Stevie's cheeks flush.

"You know, I had several friends who offered you a job. You could have rented out the condo. You could have been remarried by now to someone who has their shit together. What the fuck are you doing up here?

You're almost forty. You have fallen so far from grace. You let that man walk away, and then you what? Scurry into hiding? In *her* family's house? Have you absolutely no sense of dignity? My God, the lies I've had to tell my friends. This is getting ridiculous, Stevie. You need to pack your things—"

"And you need to get your ass out of this bar," I finally say. She stops in her tracks, sinking away from me.

"Ex*cuse* me?" she asks, putting a hand to her chest.

"I'm not going to stand here and listen to you talk to her like that. And neither is anyone else. She'll leave if she wants to leave. If she doesn't, she won't. But like you said, she's a grown woman. Seems to be doing pretty well for herself. So you can go now."

Cindy looks at me, eyes wide, lips pursed together.

Then, she looks at her daughter, who is staring back at her, chest heaving with heavy breaths.

"Fine," Cindy says, sucking her teeth. "If this is where you want to waste the rest of your pathetic life, have it. When you're done having your little mid-life crisis up here, come back down to Earth and the real world."

Then, she spins on her heel, clicking her way back through the bar, and everyone around us starts carrying on with their night like it was nothing. But when I look down at her, I see the tears welling in her eyes. I feel her body shaking, and I know it's time to go. I walk back to Nick and hand him some cash, telling him I need to get her home.

Then, I turn back to her and take her hand.

"We're gonna go home now, okay?" I ask. She doesn't say anything. She just holds onto my hand tight and follows me through the bar and to the truck.

No one is ever going to hurt you like that again, Stevie.

Not even me.

CHAPTER NINE

I FEEL his eyes on me every few seconds as I lean my head on my hand and rest it on the car door.

"Hey," he finally says. I draw in a slow breath, the tears still pricking at the backs of my eyes. Slowly, I turn to him. "You okay? You wanna talk about it?"

I think for a minute, then close my eyes. I shake my head slowly.

No. No, I don't.

"She's used to me being a convenience in her life. She's not sure what to do now that I'm inconvenient. Now that I'm not bringing anything valuable to her." I close my eyes and swallow. Then, I turn back to him. "Can tonight just be good? I...I don't want to give her this win. I want to take this night back from her," I ask him. "Today was...today was such a good day. I just... I just want tonight to be good." He looks at me, then the road, then me. Then, he slides his hand across the seat to mine and covers it. He weaves his fingers through mine, then lifts my hand to his lips. He kisses each knuckle gently, then looks back at me.

"Yeah," he says. "Tonight can just be good."

He pulls the truck into the driveway slowly, and I feel my heart rate starting to pick up as soon as he puts it in park. He makes me feel warm, like it's down to my bones. Even after the shitshow that is my mother, I still feel it with him. Like my mind can quiet, and I can just be. And I don't want it to end. I swallow as he turns to me.

"It got cold quick," I say, rubbing my arms. He nods.

"That happens this time of year," he says, looking out his windshield toward the water. "The cold rolls in off the water and just stays." He looks toward the house. "Have you used the fireplace yet?"

I nod.

"A few times."

He cocks an eyebrow.

"But have you really *used* it? Ya know, the way a local would?"

I smile.

"Is there a special way to light a fire?" I ask. "A special Blue Bay way?"

He nods, his eyebrows up.

"Yes," he says. "There's a fire, and then there's a *fire.*"

I laugh.

"Well then, in that case, do you mind showing me how to light it the right way? I'm gonna need it tonight, I think."

He tips his imaginary hat again.

"I'd be happy to. We can't have you freezing to death," he says, opening his door and hopping out.

He waits for me to walk around to the other side of the truck and unlocks the door. And as I feel the heat from his body right behind mine, my heart beats even faster. Heat flips my belly and pools between my legs as I get the door open and walk inside. He closes it behind us and walks past me toward the fireplace as I put my purse down and take his jacket off.

I walk into the room and watch as he positions the logs in a criss-cross pattern, then uses the lighter to light them in different spots. They catch quick, and he pokes them before closing the metal liner and backing away, clapping the dust from his hands.

"Well, that was fast," I say. He looks up at me as he stands to his feet. The house is small, but the chill is real. It becomes very apparent that the house is over a hundred years old on nights like this. The floors feel cold beneath my feet, and I shiver as a cool breeze seeps through the old doors.

He looks at me.

"Still cold?" he asks. I nod.

"Can't seem to warm up," I say. He takes a few steps toward me until he's directly in front of me.

"You know, when I get cold like that, a hot bath helps," he says. I swallow as he peers down at me. I feel this shift in the air between us, and suddenly, I don't feel as cold.

"Oh yeah?" I ask.

"Yeah," he whispers. He leans down so his lips are right next to my ear. "Wait here."

He walks around me and up the stairs to the landing where the bathroom is. I hear the creaking of the faucet, and then I hear the water start to run. A few moments later, he appears at the top of the stairs and waves me up to him. I can hear my heart beating in my ears, but my feet move involuntarily, as if they're not waiting for my brain to come up with a reason not to listen to him. When I reach the landing, he takes my hand and leads me into the bathroom slowly. He turns to me and pushes the door closed behind me, then takes my hands in his, his eyes locked on mine. I swallow again. I'm sure at this point he can *see* my heart beating out of my chest. He gently lifts my arms and reaches for the hem of my shirt, pulling it up over my head. Then, he moves toward my jeans, unbuttoning and unzipping them without breaking eye contact. He tugs gently to get them down over my ass, and before I know it, I'm standing in front of Cash Becker in my panties and bra.

He reaches around me slowly, unclasping my bra with one hand and letting it slide down off my arms. My nipples are hard and peaked, and I watch as his eyes graze over them before he looks back at me. He slides his hands down my sides, leaving a trail of chills in their wake as he reaches the top of my panties. His breath shudders as he takes a step closer, and suddenly, I *feel* him. Like, *him*. I feel how hard he is as he presses against me. Then, he hooks his thumbs into the sides of them and gently pulls them down.

Shaky breaths ripple through my body as I close my eyes. I wait for the touch, the kiss, *something*, but it doesn't come. Instead, I feel his breath on my ear again.

"Get in the water, Stevie," he whispers. My eyes flash open, and I stare at him for a moment. *Seriously?* I take his outstretched hand as he helps me in the tub. I sit down and lie back, letting the hot water cover me. "Good girl," he whispers, and I feel that heat between my legs again. I almost moan out loud.

Once the water reaches my shoulders, he shuts it off, then sits down on the floor next to the tub. He rolls up a towel and gently lifts my head to put it behind me.

I lie still for a few moments, eyes closed. But then, I can't take it. My impatience and my libido can't take it anymore.

It's been a *very* long time. He's awoken the kitty, and I don't want this going to waste. I haven't felt this sexually charged in...well, ever.

I open one eye and look at him, and I see him smirk.

"What's on your mind, Stevie?" he asks, his voice low and deep.

I sigh.

"Honestly?" I ask. He nods. "This isn't how I thought this was gonna go."

He lifts an eyebrow, that shit-eating grin still on his face.

"Oh?" he asks, pulling a knee up to his chest. "And how did you think it was gonna go?"

I sigh and roll my eyes.

"Nevermind," I say, growing frustrated, both sexually and the other kind.

He chuckles, then leans in over the tub so our faces are just inches apart.

"Tell me, Stevie," he says, his voice more serious, more demanding. "What did you want to happen?"

I swallow as my eyes find his.

"I... I..." I say, and suddenly, I'm nervous again. The nervous, flustered energy I feel around him is something I haven't felt any other time in my life. I guess you could compare it to teenage love—that universe-stopping, stomach-flipping kind of feeling. But it's compacted by a *very* adult sex drive.

"Did you want me to touch you?" he asks. I swallow again and nod slowly. "Where?" He takes a finger and traces my jawline with it, then down to my neck. He drags it slowly, down past my collarbone and stops between my breasts. He drags it through the water till it's resting on one of them. "Here?"

I nod. His finger dips lower in the water to my nipple, circling it under the hot water until it's peaked and pointed and hard. Then, he moves the finger to my other breast. "And here?" I nod again. Then, he looks up at me. "Did you want me to taste you?"

My heart is racing so fast I feel like I'm going to faint in this water. But still, I nod.

"Did you want my tongue to circle these? Suck on them? Bite them?" he asks. I nod. Then, his finger drags down between my breasts again, toward my belly button, then past it. Then, he stops just above my pussy. "And what about here?" he says, his finger resting gently on my pubic bone. He draws a slow circle on it as his eyes bore into mine. I nod slowly, and he gets up on both knees, leaning closer to me. "Tell me, Stevie. Tell me right now what you wanted."

I swallow and look at him, that heat between my legs now hotter than the damn water.

"I...I wanted you to taste...*me.*"

His eyes widen and dance with delight, but he doesn't take them off me.

"Taste *what?*"

I clear my throat, and at the same time, his finger slides down toward my slit, resting ever so lightly on my clit. I lean my head back slowly, my eyes closing. Then, he slides his hand farther down and quickly puts two fingers inside of me, making me cry out and bite my lip. "Taste *what,* Stevie?" he asks again.

"My pussy," I say. "I want you to taste my pussy."

His fingers move in slow motion but in a steady, circular pace inside me, and I feel the storm brewing in my body.

"Get out of this tub right now," he growls in my ear, "and I will give you what you want."

My eyes spring open as he pulls his fingers from me. Our eyes meet just as he slides them into his mouth, and I swear to God, I almost pass out. I put my hands on either side of the tub and push up, and he holds up a towel. I go to take it, but he doesn't let me. Instead, he rubs and dabs at me, then lays the towel on the sink. Then, he walks behind me, picking me up, and carries me up the second flight of stairs to the bedroom. He pushes the door open and walks to the bed, laying me down gently. I run my hand up my navel, then bite down on my finger as I look up at him, waiting for what's next.

"I want to see you," I say to him, eyeing him up and down. He smirks down at me as he steps closer.

"Soon," he says. "But we need to take care of some things first."

I raise an eyebrow.

"Like what?"

"Like you," he says. His hands start at my ankles, then move up both of my legs at the same time. And as he slides up them, he gently pushes them apart. I am so exposed right now, naked in all my glory, pussy opened wide. But it doesn't feel vulnerable. It feels powerful. It feels sexy. "Now," he says, "tell me again. What did you want?"

I moan and close my eyes.

"You," I say.

"Ah, ah," he says, reaching for my chin and tilting my head toward his. "You're gonna tell me what *you* want. And then, I'm gonna give it to you. But you need to be a good girl and use your words."

Jesus Fucking Christ, that's hot.

"I want your mouth on me," I say. "On my pussy."

He lays my legs on the bed and steps between them. Then, he puts a hand on either side of my head and bends down so our noses are only centimeters apart.

"Oh, you're gonna have that, baby," he says. "But first, I'm gonna kiss you."

And then, he does. His lips on mine, so intense it almost hurts. Our tongues crash into each other, and we suck and bite on each other's lips until they're swollen and puffy. This is different than the kiss at the lighthouse.

This feels like it *has* to happen. Like we both need it. Like our bodies have been starving for it.

We finally come apart, and he looks down at me.

"Good God, you're a beautiful woman, Stevie Rhodes," he says. My eyebrows knit together, and I feel my cheeks flush. "And I am going to spend the rest of the night making sure you know that."

He trails kisses down my neck, biting my collar bone, then sucking one nipple into his mouth while he circles and tugs on the other. He draws a line with his tongue between them, kissing my stomach and hips until he gets to my center. He puts a hand on either of my hamstrings, pushing them apart and holding them up slightly. Then, he runs his nose down my slit, and I feel myself get wetter by the second. I squeeze the comforter and press my head back into the bed, bracing for impact.

"Look at me, Stevie," he says, and I slowly open my eyes. "Watch me while I devour you."

Holy. Fucking. Shit.

And then, he does.

He starts with a long, slow kiss. Then, he sucks one lip into his mouth, then the other. His tongue slides up and down my folds, then goes in and out of me before climbing back up to my clit. His eyes are on fire as he sucks my clit into his mouth, rolling his tongue over it in a rhythmic motion that makes me pant like a fucking dog.

"Oh...oh my God, Cash," I say. "Cash...*Cash,*" I say, warning him. I feel the orgasm building in my belly, and I know it won't be long. As badly as I've been pining for this man, I'm surprised I've lasted this long. And this is *so* much better than I could have imagined.

"What's wrong, baby?" he asks, a devilish tone to his voice. I pant again and grasp for the pillows, the sheets, the comforter.

"I'm gonna...I'm..." I say. "Oh...oh..." I say again as he continues playing and sucking on my clit.

"You're gonna what, baby?" he asks. "Tell me." But when I don't answer, I feel him slide a finger inside of me without taking his mouth off of me. Then another finger. Then, they start pumping in and out of me while he separates me with his tongue. "You're gonna *what,* baby?"

"I'm...oh...I'm gonna come," I tell him. "I'm gonna come all over you if you don't move."

Much to my dismay, he completely pauses for a minute, looking at me with an intense stare.

"Listen to me, Stevie," he says. "You better come all over my fucking face. Do you hear me? Can you be a good girl and do that for me?"

His voice is stern and serious, but I can barely concentrate. All I know is, I need his mouth back on me. Like, yesterday. I nod, and I feel his fingers start to move again. "Words, Stevie. I need to know you hear me."

"Yes. I'll...oh...I'll come on you."

His head drops back down again as he circles me with his tongue, then sucks me back into his mouth. I feel myself pulsing inside as he sucks, and then it's here. The most soul-snatching orgasm I've ever had. I reach a hand down and push his head into me further as it rips through me, and I feel my wetness squirting out of me and onto him. My legs shake as he lays them down gently, his eyes raising to mine again. Then, he juts his tongue out and licks his lips as he stares down at me.

"Oh, my," I manage to mutter, heavy breaths still heaving in my chest. I drape an arm over my face, but he reaches a hand down and pulls it from me.

"No quitting just yet," he says. "That was just the appetizer. I have more to give you."

I open my eyes and look up at him, then with the last bit of energy I have left, I push myself up from the bed and stand in front of him, my wetness dripping onto my thighs. I take his hand and put it between my legs.

"I think you've given me enough," I say. "It's my turn." But as I reach for his belt buckle, he takes my hands again.

"Stevie," he whispers, bringing my hands to his lips and kissing them gently. "You don't know what you've already done for me. Just being here. I'm going to enjoy this next part," he says, "but tonight, let me make you feel good. Let me show you how beautiful you are. Let me handle this, okay?"

I swallow.

I've never been dominated like this.

I've never wanted to be.

But with him, I feel the need for control leave my

body. I feel myself loosening the moment he touches me. I feel my muscles relaxing, my jaw unclenching. I feel myself getting hornier by the second, but that's about it.

Everything else feels lighter.

Like I'm in good hands.

His hands.

I nod as he reaches down and pulls his shirt up over his head. His big, broad shoulders are even more beautiful than I imagined, his tan skin spackled in a few small smatterings of freckles stretched across them. Then, he reaches into his pocket, snagging a condom from his wallet. He unzips his pants and lets them fall down, his boxers along with them. And then, he's naked in front of me, looking like a Greek god of some sort, his dark hair disheveled, his beard glistening with my wetness.

He pushes me back down gently and tears the condom open with his teeth. He rolls it on and then takes a step toward me. He licks the pads of his fingers, circling my entrance. But I'm nice and wet from his first go-round still, and my entire body is pulling toward him.

"What do you want, baby?" he whispers as he puts a hand on either side of my head again. I reach up and wrap my hands around his wrists.

"I want you inside of me," I tell him, wasting no time with being shy anymore. I know what I want, and I want it *now*.

"Good girl." He smiles, then holds my legs steady as he plunges inside of me, making my whole body go straight. He's big, and he's *deep*. And then, he lets out a low, throaty moan, and I see stars.

"Oh, fuck," I cry out as he starts to move, in and out, holding my legs in the air like he's steering something. He fucks me hard and fast, moving in and out of me, stretching me around him. Then, he holds tight to my hips as he plows into me once more before pulling out quickly. He flips me to my stomach and pulls me toward the edge of the bed, then slides a hand under my body and pushes my body up so that I'm on my knees, facing away from him. He enters me from behind, and I reach an arm up and around his head. I feel his breath on my neck, hear him moaning as he strokes, and then I feel his other hand find my clit again.

"Come with me?" he asks, and I nod as I moan in sync with his every motion. His hand moves in tandem with his strokes, and then finally, I see stars again.

"I'm there, Cash," I tell him. "I'm there...I'm..." And then my legs go stiff as he grunts behind me, and I feel him go rigid, too. He slides out of me, then falls on top of me. We lie together for a moment, our bodies slick with each other's sweat as we try to slow our breathing down. He rolls off me and onto his side so we're facing each other.

He reaches a hand out and pushes a loose strand of hair off my face.

"Good God, you're beautiful, woman," he whispers to me, and I feel my cheeks flush. The man just had me cracked open like a clam, but I get shy when he compliments me. I shake my head, but his face stays serious.

"Listen to me, Stevie." I swallow. "You are the most beautiful woman I have ever met in my life. And you deserve so much good in your life. Don't forget that, okay? Promise me you won't forget it."

I swallow again, but it feels a little harder this time.

"Okay," I say, even though I'm not sure my heart is completely in it. He reaches an arm around me and pulls me into him.

"Just know that you've brought more good to my life in the short time you've been in it than I ever thought I could find."

We get cleaned up, and I feel the nerves building in my belly. He walks out of the bathroom and back up the stairs, and we stare at each other for a minute.

"I'm gonna sleep with you now. Is that alright?" he asks.

A silly smile plays across my lips. *Thank God.* I nod.

"Yes, please."

"Okay, good. You can't rock my world like that and then send me packing," he says as he walks toward me and takes my hand. "Besides, I have something really important to do tomorrow morning."

I look up at him as we climb into the bed and get under the covers.

"What's that?"

"Wake up next to you."

CHAPTER TEN

THE SKY IS that deep gray-blue it gets when the light is trying to crack its way through but hasn't quite made it yet. It's enough for me to sneak out of the bed and take a piss without crashing into everything and waking her, but not enough light to make her stir yet. Thank God. I'm not done yet.

I slither back into the bed and under the covers, back to the spot I left. She's got her hands folded underneath her head like a fucking little angel. Her breaths are short and sharp, her face totally calm. Not a worry line or scrunched brow to be seen. I smile as I graze my hand over her cheek, careful not to actually make contact. I've been awake for a little while now—I'm a light sleeper—and she woke me a little bit ago, saying, "No," in her sleep. That was it, just "No." I almost woke her, but she calmed back down.

So, now I'm just sitting here, staring at this beautiful woman in front of me who seems totally at peace. And watching as she slowly becomes mine.

I think about the way her mom looked at her. The disgust in her eyes. And I think about what kind of shithead could ever think of Stevie that way. It was so apparent by the way she carried herself that she felt Stevie was there to serve her. That the direction Stevie was taking *her* life wasn't suiting her mom. Cindy. I'd like to have another word or two with her. I was nice at that bar last night. I didn't want to overstep, seeing as I've known her daughter for a month. But it took all my strength not to tell her to get her plastic ass out of Maine and never come back.

I think about all the shit Stevie's been through over the last year. Having her husband get a cancer diagnosis. Realizing he was in love with someone else. Having the strength to end it, knowing she was going to be the one to be by herself.

I keep thinking about that one thing her mom said before she left.

"When you're done having your little mid-life crisis up here, come back down to Earth and the real world."

My stomach lurches as the thought of this—*us*—just being an escape for her. But that's one thing I've learned about Stevie. She doesn't shy away from the hard shit. She takes it.

I just don't want her to anymore.

I want to take the hits for her. I want her to know what it's like to be the center of the fucking universe.

I stare at her, completely overwhelmed by my own emotions, and I realize what is happening.

It's something that hasn't happened since I was seventeen years old.

It's something I've avoided like the plague ever since.

But I'm fucking falling in love with her.

You don't deserve this. You don't deserve her.

The last time I was in love with someone, I lost everything. Almost my life. Almost hers. Almost everything and anything that ever mattered.

You. Do. Not. Deserve. Her.

I shake my head to clear the thoughts before they take over.

Because right now, in this perfect moment, I feel like maybe she deserves *me.*

She might not know it, but she's mine, this one.

And I will love her like she is.

A little more time passes, and the room slowly fills with more light. Finally, she starts to blink, and I smile. I stroke her jaw with my thumb. I kiss her forehead, her cheek, her nose, her lips.

"Good morning," she whispers as she smiles back.

"Good morning, beautiful," I say. I lean down for one more forehead kiss, then I slide out of the bed. Her brows furrow. I lean back over the bed and kiss her. "Don't worry. I'm not going anywhere. Come downstairs in ten minutes, okay?"

She smiles again as she pulls the sheets up a little further on her naked body. I dress quickly, then go downstairs to the kitchen. I start the coffee, scramble the eggs, and pop some toast into the toaster. I throw a few pieces of bacon in another skillet just as she's coming down the last step. She's wearing my jacket again, and the sight of her in my clothes has me reeling all over again. She's so fucking beautiful. And when she's wearing my clothes, when she looks like me, smells like me, it feels like she's *mine*. Just how I like her. I push the eggs around just as the coffee finishes brewing and scoot to pull the pot off the burner. I fill one of the dark-red mugs from the cabinet, add a little bit of cream, just like she likes it, and I hand it to her. I kiss her cheek.

"Go sit on the porch," I tell her. "I'll be right there." She smiles up at me, and I feel my knees go weak like I'm some sort of teenage boy.

"Mmm," she says as the coffee hits her soul. "Okay."

After a few more minutes, once the house successfully smells like bacon and I have two decent-looking plates made, I carry them out, along with my mug, and sit next to her on the wicker bench that faces the water.

She's rubbing her hands together when I walk outside, so I put the plates down, run back inside and grab the throw off the couch, and run back out. I lay it across our laps and scoot closer to her so she gets some of my heat, too. Then, we eat our breakfast in silence as we watch the last few moments of the sunrise and watch the tide roll away.

"Mmm," she says after a few minutes, putting her empty plate on the table in front of us and curling her legs up underneath us. "So, is this the Cash Becker Treatment?"

I raise an eyebrow as I take another sip of coffee and put my mug down. I slide my plate next to hers, then stretch my arm around her.

"The what?"

She giggles.

"Bed *and* breakfast?" she asks. I shake my head as I pinch her side and nuzzle her neck.

"You deserve the fucking world," I whisper to her, and her face grows a little more serious. She rests her head on my shoulder, and I lay mine on hers. We look out over the water as I pull her legs across my lap and tug the blanket higher up on us.

"I had four miscarriages," she whispers. Before I look at her, I draw in a slow breath. My heart rate picks up, and then it feels like the whole thing splinters in my chest. I tighten my grip around her, waiting for her to go on. "I was in my thirties when we got married. My mom warned me that I needed to start trying right away, but we wanted to wait a few years. And then, it turns out, she was right."

Fuck you, Cindy, I think.

"The second one, I had to have a D&C," she says. I close my eyes for a moment. "And when my mom walked into the room after the procedure, the first thing she said was, 'I told you not to wait, honey.'" I say nothing, but my hands ball into fists. "Cade was understanding. Actually, he was maybe a little *too* understanding." I raise my eyebrow. I know I have no right to get all tight and bothered when she mentions his name, but I do. "He said all the right things—at least, in theory. He'd reassure me all the time that if we never got pregnant, it would be fine. That he was content with us. He didn't really feel like anything was missing." She pauses, and I realize that a tear is rolling down her cheek. I lift my thumb to swipe it away. "I know he said it to make me feel better. But all I really felt was alone. Because *I* wasn't fine. I wanted kids. I wanted my fucking body to work the way it was supposed to—the way my mother reminded me every chance she got that hers had." She pauses for a minute to sniff and wipe her nose with her napkin. "After the fourth one, I told him I was done. I went to a specialist and had an exploratory procedure done. Turns out, I had stage four endometriosis."

I lift another eyebrow. She smiles faintly, knowing I don't know what it means.

"It's a, uh…feminine issue that can make it hard to have kids. The doctors said that after looking at my uterus, there was no chance I was ever going to get pregnant. They said based on how advanced it was, I had had it for years. It had nothing to do with my age after all. After that, I decided to have a hysterectomy. I decided that if I couldn't make my body do what I wanted it to, then I was going to take some control back."

I swallow.

"And did you feel like you succeeded?" I ask her, stroking her hair. She's quiet for a minute, and I feel her shoulders start to shake with little sobs that tear me apart. I pull her into my chest, kissing the top of her head.

"No," she says between sobs. We don't say anything else for a few moments. She collects herself, and then she sits up. "I've never said that before, because I wanted to believe that it was on *my* terms. On *my* authority. But no. I feel sad. A little empty sometimes. And I'm fucking mad. I don't want kids now. I'm happy with where I am, on my own."

I shrink back a bit at that choice of words, but I let it go.

"But sometimes, I wish I wasn't broken. I think I would have been good at it," she says.

I stroke her hair a few more times and kiss her forehead.

"You would have," I tell her. "I know that because of the way you want to make sure everyone else is happy. The way that this whole experience," I say, motioning to the cottage and space around us, "seems like it's so foreign to you. Running off and doing something for you? Something to help *you* heal, regardless of what other people think about it? It didn't take long to see that that's something you've never done. But I'm so fucking glad you did, Stevie. And you know what? It's okay to be sad about it. It's okay to be angry and hate the world. You don't *always* have to rise with the sun, Stevie. You don't have to be the light everywhere you go for every person you meet. You're allowed to want some quiet time in the dark every now and then, too. You can just *be*."

She looks up at me, her big blue eyes bloodshot and filled with tears, and I pull her face to mine, kissing them away.

"And you know something else, Stevie Rhodes? You might think you're broken," I tell her, kissing her gently on her lips, "but I think you're the reason I'm starting to feel fixed."

She closes her eyes and bites her lip to stop it from trembling, and I stroke her cheeks again with my thumbs, pressing my forehead to hers and begging her with my eyes and my touch to look at me. Finally, she does.

This is it.

She has to know.

"I've done some bad things in my life, Stevie," I tell her, my own voice starting to crack now. "I have no idea what you want the rest of your life to look like. And I truly don't know if I deserve you. But if you stay, I'll do my damndest to become a version of me that does. I want you to be my Sunshine Stevie. But not in the moronic way the assholes before made you to be. You're my sunshine because my whole fucking world has started to revolve around you. I can't sleep without knowing where you are. I can't breathe if it's been too long since I've seen you. You are the center of my universe, Stevie."

Her eyes widen as she pushes up off my chest. She turns so her body is angled toward me. She doesn't say a single word. She just falls into me, her lips crashing into mine, her soul taking hold of mine in the same exact moment.

CHAPTER ELEVEN

stevie

IT'S BEEN a few weeks since the incident with my mom, and he has barely left my side, except to work. It's official that sleeping with him is one of my new favorite pastimes. I don't mean sex—although, he's pretty fucking fantastic at that, too—but actually sleeping. When I wake in the middle of the night for whatever reason—whether it's a bad dream, anxiety, or the fact that I have to pee *all* the time now—I look at his face, I feel his body, the way his hands find me even when he's asleep, and I drift back so much easier than without him.

Blue Bay has gotten its first big snows of the season, and every time it falls, I become a child. I stop what I'm doing to run to the window, and he laughs at me, joining me, watching it with me.

It's all like a fucking fairy tale.

I never want it to end.

I'm working at the kitchen counter when he comes

down the stairs, wearing a pair of jeans and a sweat jacket that's unzipped. He's not wearing a shirt underneath it, so it's just his big, beautiful chest in all its glory.

"Mmm," I say out loud, licking my lips. He laughs and shakes his head as he bends down and kisses me.

"I'm officially out of clothes," he says, shrugging as he slides my coffee across the counter and takes a sip of it. "I may *actually* need to go home today."

I gasp and cover my mouth.

"*What?*" I feign shock, and he smiles. But there's a small piece of me that really doesn't want him to go. I guess it's because there is a small piece of me that's worried that if he leaves, he won't come back.

He kisses me again, slower this time, my chin between his pointer finger and thumb.

"You can't get rid of me that easily," he says, almost like he's reading my mind. "I want to take you somewhere tonight."

I smile. I love when he makes plans for us. I'm usually the planner. Always have been. I've always done what people expected of me—and then some.

But with him, I can just exist, sipping my coffee in my yoga pants while he pulls me deeper and deeper into his world.

"Somewhere sounds great," I say, taking a sip of my coffee. He kisses my lips, then my cheek, then my neck, and I slink back under his ticklish touch.

"I'll be back around five," he says. "Pack a bag."

Now, he has my attention. I raise an eyebrow.

"A bag?"

He nods on his way out the door.

"Just for one night," he says. Then, he winks. "Nothing fancy. See you later."

And then I'm left to the slowest fucking Friday in the history of the world.

Finally, the clock strikes five, and per usual, he is right on time. I hear his boots in the gravel, and when he walks in, I can't help but smile. I close my laptop and look up at him.

"*Finally,*" I say. "Gimme five, and I'll be ready."

He holds up his hands.

"Take your time. No rush, baby."

I melt.

A long time ago, I convinced myself that I was too old, too mature for pet names. Cade and I never really used them, and instead of digging into why, I just chocked it up to being something that wasn't "us." Something we didn't need to be happy.

Boy, did I have another thing coming.

I run up the stairs and grab a t-shirt to sleep in. I pack a clean pair of underwear, a sweatshirt and jeans for the morning, and my warm boots. I grab my toothbrush, my comb, and a scrunchie, and throw everything in my duffel bag. I zip it up, fluff my hair in the mirror, and make my way back downstairs. He's just sitting there on the couch, smiling, looking like he belongs— both in this cottage, and with me.

He stands up and takes my bag from me.

"Let's go, pretty lady," he says, taking my hand and walking me out the door. He locks it behind us, then helps me into the truck, handing me my bag. He gets back in on his side, starts it up, and we take off. He slides one hand across the center console and grips my thigh while he drives, and I lean my head back against the seat. After a few minutes, I recognize the roads that we're taking, and I turn to him.

"Are we going back to Glassy Point?" I ask excitedly, and he turns to me and smiles, nodding.

"I'm glad you're excited," he says. "I thought it might be old news."

I shoot him a look.

"You kidding me? That's my *place*," I say with a sly grin. He laughs and gives my thigh a squeeze just as we approach the tree tunnel. He parks, and I'm pleased that today does not appear to be a day it's open to the public again. Just us.

But then I realize, it's fucking Christmas Eve.

That's why no one is here.

It's fucking Christmas, and I didn't even realize it.

"You okay?" he asks, sensing my mind is somewhere else.

I smile quickly and nod.

"Yeah, yeah," I say. "I just…I totally forgot what day it was until right now. I've never spent a Christmas without…family. Or not at home. Just…different."

He lifts my hand and kisses it.

"How about we make it a good different?" he asks.

He turns the truck off and reaches for our bags in the backseat, and I give him a look.

"Wait. Is this where we're staying?" I ask. He smiles and shrugs his shoulders, then slides out of the truck. I follow him to the side door as he unlocks it and waits for me to get inside before he closes it. It's chilly in here, and he turns up the stairwell lights, standing aside for me to go. The first thing I notice when we get to the top of the tower is that everything feels fresh and clean. There's a vase of fresh flowers, and all the shades are opened so that what's left of the daylight can seep in. On the table at the back of the room sits two place settings and a big brown carryout bag. There's a candle burning at the center of the table, and I turn to him.

"Did you set all this up?" I ask. He smiles.

"Chuck owed me a solid," he says. Then, he sets his bag down and opens it, pulling out folded sheets and a big, blue blanket. "This way, we know for a fact they're fresh," he says, and I smile. "There's a bathroom in the building next door, and it's connected by a door down-stairs under the stairwell. It's not the Four Seasons, but I wanted to see it with you at night. Is this okay?"

I walk up to him slowly, wrapping my arms around his neck and pressing up onto my tiptoes.

"No one has ever done something like this for me before," I tell him. It seems so simple. In some people's terms, this might be no better than glamping. No actual indoor plumbing in the room we're in, the chill of a century-old building, the lack of light.

But it's his place, and he's sharing it with me. It's

his place that he's now let become *my* place, and there's something so overwhelming about it.

"I can't wait to stay here with you," I whisper before I pull him in for a long kiss. But as we do, there's a shift in the air. It goes from a playful, grateful mood, to one of hunger. One of pining for one another. And we need each other *now*. I let my tongue slide in and out of his mouth, nibbling on his bottom lip before I slide one hand between us and let it rest over his crotch. I feel the bulge, and I smile as he now takes my bottom lip into his mouth. There's something so satisfying about knowing that this, his arousal, his desire, is all for me.

I grip him through his jeans, then slide my other hand down to unbuckle and unzip them. I take his shirt off over his head, and he does the same to me. He tugs my pants down, leaving just my panties on, and he lets his own jeans fall to the ground and swipes them out of the way with his foot. He picks me up, and I wrap my legs around his waist as he carries me across the room, and I wrap my arms tighter around his neck. I love the sensation of his bare skin on mine. Like our hearts sync when they touch, like our blood pumps in the same rhythm. He knows what I want before I do. He presses me up against the wall first, the bare bricks cool against my back as he kisses my lips, my neck, my collar bone. Then, he slides me up a few inches, sucking one nipple into his mouth as I clutch my legs around him tighter. He lets his tongue flick it and play with it, then lets his teeth graze it as it slowly slides out of his mouth. I feel that heat between my legs, and I am full-on craving him now.

I try to slide my hand down to him again, but he shifts in place, wrapping one hand under each of my thighs. Then, to my surprise, with his sheer fucking strength, he pushes me up farther so I'm sitting on his shoulders. Except, we're facing opposite directions, so his face is directly angled at my pussy.

"Oh, my God," I say as I look down at him. He looks up at me, kissing the insides of my thighs.

"Relax, baby," he says, "and hold on tight."

Then, his tongue finds my slit, and he laps at my clit nice and slow, moving up and down over top of it. I reach down and clutch his hair, pressing him into me as his mouth works its magic.

He moans beneath me, and I feel myself get wetter and wetter.

"My God, I love the way you taste, sweet girl," he says. "I literally cannot get enough of you."

He grips my ass tighter, pushing me into him as he moves his mouth over me, kissing me, sucking my folds into his mouth, massaging my clit with his tongue until I feel the orgasm building up inside of me.

"Oh, God," I say, slapping one hand against the brick behind me. "Oh, God, Cash, it's...I'm..."

He licks faster, sucking my clit into his mouth and massaging it with more pressure until my entire body goes rigid. Then, my legs go limp, dropping over his shoulders as he comes up for air. He gently slides me back down his body, holding me steady until he knows my legs are strong enough to hold me.

I catch my breath slowly, then look up at him.

"Did you...did you just..." I start to ask. Then, he smirks.

"Did I just eat you out in mid-air?" he asks. "Yes. Yes, I did. I'll go down on you, up on you, any which way you'll let me have you."

And just like that, I feel that zap between my legs again. I'm ready for round two, and I know he is, too.

"Take me, now," I tell him, and he lifts an eyebrow.

"Bossy tonight?" he asks. I step forward and slide my hand down into his boxers, squeezing his shaft in my hand and giving it hard pump after pump.

"Do it," I tell him, and the smile leaves his face as he grows thicker and harder in my hand. But as I move my hand on him, I feel that warm, familiar feeling of his pre-cum spreading out onto my hands. And now, I want a taste. I drop to my knees in front of him, yanking the boxers down and throwing them to the side. I move him toward one of the chairs and push him down, moving onto my knees between his legs. I give his cock a few more pumps with my hand before taking it into my mouth, moving my head up and down, adding suction from my lips as I do. He drops his head back, exposing his neck, his pecs and abs flexing as he moves in my mouth. God, he is so fucking beautiful. And all I want is for him to explode. I want to *make* him explode. I've never wanted it so badly for someone else, but I want it for him. I want him to fall apart because of me. I want him to lose all control because of me. And the way he moans my name and tugs on my hair as I go down on him makes my pussy wet. Because there's nothing fucking sexier than giving it to the person you love.

I reach a hand down and cradle his balls, massaging them gently in my hand as my other hand and mouth continue to work on him. A moment later, he pushes up, stroking my face.

"Baby, baby, you have to stop," he says.

I pause and scoot back, looking at him.

"I want you to cover me," I tell him, and he moans again.

"Jesus," he says. "Let me grab a condom." But as he moves to stand, I hold him down.

"I said I want you to cover me," I say again, and he looks at me, wide-eyed.

"Are…are you sure?" he asks.

I lick my lips and nod.

"My face or somewhere else on me. You choose."

He blinks and licks his lips.

"Are you sure?" he asks again.

"Is there a reason I shouldn't be?" I ask. He shakes his head.

"Me either. And I can't get pregnant, so I want you to fuck me raw."

He sits forward so we're face to face and kisses me.

"Where the hell did you come from, woman?" he whispers before he stands up, pulling me to my feet. He swipes the blanket he brought with him and lays it out on the floor, spreading it out so it's flat.

"Lie down," he says, and I do. I slide a hand down between my breasts, past my belly button, to my pussy, and swirl my fingers around it while he gets on his knees in front of me. "Let me see you," he commands, and I swallow. "Show me how you make yourself come."

So, I start moving my fingers in a circular motion, applying a little pressure as I go. And when I open my eyes, I see him stroking himself as he watches me, and I groan out loud.

"Jesus, that's so hot," I say. He smirks.

"Tell me about it," he says. Then, he scoots in closer to me and takes an ankle in each hand, spreading my legs out into a V. "You ready for me, baby?"

I nod, licking my lips, and then he plunges into me, making me gasp out loud.

"Oh," I cry out as he finds his way inside of me. Then, he starts fucking me hard, my pussy gripping him and making every thrust feel like I'm going to explode into a thousand pieces. He licks the pads of his fingers, then starts rubbing my clit in time with his pulsing inside of me, and I'm seeing stars. My back is arching, my hands are clutching at the blanket, but his grip around my ankle tightens.

"Hey," he says, "look at me."

So, I do.

"Keep your eyes on me while I make you come," he commands. "And then watch what you do to me."

So, I do.

Our eyes stay locked, and I am writhing beneath him as the orgasm builds up.

"Right there," I say. "Don't stop. Don't stop."

"Oh, I'm not stopping, baby," he assures me. "Not until you're a sopping mess."

A little late for that.

Then, I feel it, starting at my toes and rippling through my body. I dig my nails into his arms, and my legs fall straight as I scream out his name. When my legs stop shaking, he looks at me.

"My turn?" he asks. I nod.

"Yes, please," I tell him.

He fucks me a little harder, a little faster, then pulls out of me. He crawls into me closer, giving himself two or three quick pumps, and then he explodes on my stomach, covering me in him, and I want to explode all over again.

I laugh in sheer pleasure as he collapses over me, catching himself on his forearms so that he's just above me.

"I ask again," he says once he catches his breath. "Where the fuck did you come from, woman?"

A few hours later, we're lying on the blanket with the sheets around us, one pillow under both of our heads. We're facing each other, and he's tracing every edge of my face, like he's sketching it. Then, he stops.

"I forgot," he says with a snap. He rolls over toward his bag on the floor behind him and pulls something out. "I've been waiting to give you this till the right moment. This feels like it could be it. Merry Christmas."

He holds up a navy-blue string bracelet with a silver lighthouse charm dangling from it.

"Your second Blue Bay souvenir," he says. I smile and hold up my wrist so he can tie it on.

"I love this," I tell him, holding the charm between my fingers. "This is beautiful."

He kisses my lips, then my forehead.

"So are you."

CHAPTER TWELVE

STEVIE and I have basically been non-stop since the night her mom came to town. I don't want to leave her alone for her own sake, but I need it just as much. Being with Stevie is like...I don't have the word. I won't say it's a high. I've been high more than my fair share in this life. Being with Stevie isn't like that. It's like she's healing me. The feeling she gives me doesn't dissipate like a high does. I don't feel like I'm falling back down to Earth. I feel like, with every moment I spend with her, she lifts me higher. And when she leaves, I can stand on my own because of the strength loving her gives me.

When we're apart, I know it's just a part of loving her. That having someone in my life that I miss so much, even when we're only apart for a few hours, means I'm one of the luckiest sons of bitches alive.

I'm walking around the corner and going into Mickey's to pick up our coffee. The sun is bright, but the air is cold. It's extra cold for October—even up here. But I don't care. Nothing weighs me down these days.

Mickey nods as I walk in the shop, pointing to the two cups at the edge of the counter.

"Thanks, Mick," I call back to him as I reach for them, but he calls my name.

"Hang on there, son," he says. I spin back around, but his face is serious. "Hey, I wanted to tell you that one of the kids that works my evening shift mentioned this morning that someone came into the shop a few days ago asking for you."

I swallow.

"Asking for…for me?"

He nods.

I blink a few times, looking around as if that person is going to appear out of thin air.

"What did they look like? Man, woman?"

Mickey shrugs.

"I'll try and find more out," he says. "That's all I know right now. Listen, kid, I know I don't know all your dirty little secrets, and I'm not asking to. A person deserves to have a second chance. I just wanted you to know. Blue Bay's a small town. So, if someone's looking for you, there's a good chance they will eventually find you."

I nod and swallow, taking the coffees off the counter.

"Thanks, Mick. Let me know if you find out anything else."

I walk back to my truck in a hurry, get in, and put the coffees in the cup holders. This weird feeling of panic washes over me. My chest tightens. My palms get clammy. As much as I don't want to, I pick up my phone and dial my mom.

"Yeah?" she answers after a few rings. I hate the way even just her voice makes me feel.

"Mom, hey," I say, washing a hand over my face.

"Well, twice in a week, huh? To what do I owe the honor?" she says, the sarcasm and cigarette smoke thick in her voice.

"Just checking in," I lie, as if I would ever want to do that. Having fucked-up parents can fuck you up for life if you let it. I'm trying desperately to make sure that doesn't come true for me. "Hey, listen, uh...you weren't, uh, up here or anything, were you?"

There's a pause, then I hear her scoff.

"Up *there?* Why the fuck would I be up there? Just because you ran away for a fantasy doesn't mean I'm dumb enough to follow," she says.

On one hand, I'm irritated. On the other, I'm a little more unsettled than I was before I called her. If it wasn't her, who else would it be?

Mom's old boyfriends are all dead or in jail.

There could only be one person left, and...*no. Do not let yourself go there.*

It would be impossible.

I sigh and pull out of my spot in the direction of Stevie's cottage.

Just as I'm about to pull into her drive, my phone buzzes again. It's Marie.

"Hey, Marie," I say. "How's it going? I happen to be pulling up to the cottage as we speak."

"Oh, great!" she says. "Things going okay? Stevie settled in?"

I pause for a minute, watching her as she does her yoga on her lime-green mat, facing the water, unaware that I'm here or that there is any other life on the planet at this moment. God, I love watching her, her blonde locks tied up in a bun, a thick gray headband that matches her gray sweatshirt.

She's so beautiful in this light.

She's beautiful in any light.

I pull over farther back so I don't interrupt her. And so that I can watch her for a moment.

"I think so," I say. "Seems to be enjoying herself. Got the place almost winterized. I'll come back next week to check on the water lines and everything."

"Wonderful, thank you so much," she says. "So, have you, uh, gotten to know her at all?"

I smile.

"We've spent some time together," I tell her. "Yes. She's...pretty wonderful."

There's a short pause, and then she speaks.

"Oh," she says, "am I sensing a little cottage romance?"

I can't help but smile.

"I'll never tell," I laugh.

"Well, honestly, that would make me happy," she says. "She's a tough woman. And she's been through a lot. She deserves a little happiness."

I pause for a moment, remembering everything she had told me.

"Yeah, uh, she told me about the year," I say, biting my tongue.

Another pause.

"There's a lot to the story," she tells me, "probably more than even I know. So I'll just leave it at...she deserves a little happiness."

"Noted," I say. "I accept that challenge."

She laughs again.

"Good man. Thanks for keeping an eye on everything. Talk soon."

"Bye, Marie."

Maybe I don't deserve happiness, but she does.

And I intend to see that through.

CHAPTER THIRTEEN

stevie

TEN WEEKS.

It's been ten weeks to the day since I first stepped foot here in Blue Bay.

It's been ten weeks since I was accidentally naked in front of Cash. It's been around four since I was naked in front of him on purpose.

And since that night that my mom descended upon us like some sort of black cloud, we've barely spent a night apart. He stays with me most nights because he doesn't have WiFi. So, instead of having to rush home in the morning for work, we stay here at the cottage, soaking in some extra time together in the morning before I log on and he heads out for the day. He fixes up the houses during the mornings and does his handyman projects in the afternoons. And since I've been here, I've learned there is very little he doesn't know how to fix. Even if it's unorthodox, not by the book, he seems to always figure out a way to fix something that's broken.

Including me.

His friends have completely embraced me. Even Jamie seems to have gotten over the fact that we are together. She greets us both with a quick smile whenever we stop in for a bite to eat at the restaurant. She's friendly enough and usually adds in a, "See you guys next time," when we pay the bill. When we hang out as a group, she warms up to me quickly, and I've actually given her some pointers. She's taking night classes and wants to go into PR.

Mickey always has two coffees ready in the mornings now, instead of just one. Our days are so simple, really. It's just time together, work, trips to town, trips to the lighthouse. Meals together—sometimes I cook, sometimes he does. Sometimes we bag cooking altogether and get carry out.

I start most mornings with some yoga out in the grass, facing the water. And more than once, I've caught him watching me from the window or the porch. He doesn't shy away when I catch him. Our eyes lock, and he smiles. He's not ashamed. Instead, he has this look on his face that makes my whole body shiver. Like he's just so fucking happy. So proud. I've never looked at someone and realized how much they cared about me until I got here with him. Not with my mother. Not with Cade.

No one.

But when I see him, when I catch him looking at me, it's this undeniable, overwhelming, gut-punch of a realization. This is a man who is in love. And he's in love with me.

The craziest part is that I'm in love with him, too.

Two months and some change. That's it. That's all it took. It's a fast love, that's for sure. In my past, I've been slow, calculated. I've taken my time, made one hundred percent certain on every major decision in my life. No mistakes.

And look where that got me.

Alone at forty with no plan.

Until I found him. Unexpectedly, out of nowhere. This fast, deep love. A love I didn't think about. A love that just came into my life like a falling star, lighting up my whole world. Out of my control, out of my element. But I've never felt anything like it.

Neither of us have said it. I haven't had this overwhelming feeling to proclaim it yet. Maybe I will. But I think that might be the most beautiful part about it. I feel it *from* him as intensely as I feel it *for* him. I look at him, and I just know that he loves me as much as I love him. That we only know bits and pieces about each other, but we embrace it all, knowing there is more to come.

I'm finishing up on my yoga mat outside when I hear the door open and close. I look up at him as he smiles down at me, crouching down next to me.

"God, you're a beautiful woman," he says before he leans onto his hands and kisses me. "Do you have plans tonight?" he asks. I smirk.

"You know damn well that *you* are my plans in this town," I say. He laughs. "That's it. You."

He puts his hands on his knees and pushes himself to stand, reaching a hand down to me.

"Excellent," he says. "Then, in that case, we have plans tonight."

I take his hand, and he yanks me up, wrapping his big arms around my waist and lifting my feet off the ground. I wrap my arms around his neck and kiss him.

"Ya know what? I think I'm busy," I say with a sly smile. He pinches my sides, and I cry out in laughter as he nuzzles into my neck and spins me around.

"My ass," he says, finally setting me down. "I'll be here around six." Then, he steals another kiss and heads off in the direction of his truck.

My work day drags on even though I'm pretty busy. I had a presentation this morning, some numbers to go over, and a few conference calls I sat in on, but I finally send off my last email and shut my computer down. I stand up and stretch, walking toward the window to take in the last few minutes of daylight before I head upstairs to get ready. I take a hot shower, dry and curl my hair, put some makeup on, and pull a sweater out of my bag. I pull on my favorite pair of jeans—the ones that make my ass look the best—and slip on a pair of gray booties. I give myself one more onceover in the mirror just as I hear the front door open.

"Hey, beautiful," I hear him call out just as a huge smile crosses my lips, and I walk down the steps. He stops in his tracks and takes me in, his eyes scanning me from head to toe. He sucks his teeth and smiles. "God damn, I'm a lucky man."

I cross the living room and press up onto my toes, kissing him long and hard. Before he lets me go, he presses his forehead to mine for a moment, his eyes closed, his arms locked around me tight. And we just stand there.

"Okay," he finally says, breaking the silence, "we better go before I take all your clothes off and we never make it out the damn door." He slides his hand down and squeezes my ass, and I laugh as he kisses me one last time.

A few minutes later, he's parking the truck on a side street downtown and helping me out. He doesn't let go of my hand, and I fucking love the way it feels when he does this. It's natural, but it still feels so fresh and new. He's claimed me. I'm his.

We walk a little ways, the cold wind making chills spring up on my skin, and he wraps an arm around my shoulders as we get to Dunny's. I look up at him and smile as he stops to pull the door open.

"'The spot where the men take their ladies when they want to impress them,'" I quote him from the first day we went out together. He smiles and shrugs.

"I was sorta hoping you forgot that," he says with a chuckle. I smile up at him again.

"I don't think there's a single thing about you I've forgotten since we met."

He checks in at the hostess stand, and she takes us back to a private table tucked in the back corner of the restaurant. The lights are dimmed, and everything is pretty quiet. The table is tucked next to a big floor-to-ceiling window, and I can see the lights from the boats and houses out across the water. We fill up on wine and artisan breads and amazing lobster and filets until I feel like I'm going to explode. After a little while longer, he pays the bill, and we're standing to leave. He puts his hand on my lower back, guiding me toward the door. He jumps in front of me to get it, then takes my hand as we get outside. He kisses me once before we start walking, then again once he wraps his arm around my neck.

When I'm with him, I don't feel like I'm on the "wrong" side of thirty-five. I don't feel like forty is creeping around the corner—or maybe I do. But I'm not afraid of it. I'm not trying to avoid it. I feel ready for it. For whatever is coming. Because he is. He loves what is right in front of him. He gets excited by what I am when I roll over and look at him every day. Not by what he thinks I *could* be. I'm not constantly running to catch up with a version of myself that I think he wants me to be. I feel like I can breathe.

As we approach the truck, he swings me around so we're facing each other. He grips my hips and pulls me into him, kissing me harder. Then, he bends down to my ear.

"I cannot fucking wait to get you out of this sweater," he says, and I feel my stomach twist and turn and flip. I kiss him again slowly, biting his bottom lip.

I swear, I could do this forever with him.

I giggle nervously, sliding my hand down to graze his crotch. His eyes dance, but then we both freeze when someone calls his name.

A woman.

"Cash Becker?" we hear the voice say. From the front of his truck, a young woman—*really* young—early twenties, walks around till she's just a few feet away from us. Her eyes bounce back and forth from me, to him, to me, back to him. I swallow.

Great, I think. Another blast from his past. Except, this one is even younger.

But there's something about Cash's face that doesn't quite say *old flame.* Instead, he looks confused.

"Yes?" he says. "Have we met?"

Her eyes stay locked on him, and she steps up onto the curb so we are just feet apart.

"No, we haven't," the woman says. "But my name is Eden. And I'm your daughter."

My first reaction is that it's some kind of weird mistake. I look at Cash, trying to gauge his expression. I'm expecting to see some sort of look on his face that confirms my suspicions. That this is some weird prank or mix-up. But instead, he looks like a ghost. His eyes are big and wide, and he swallows as he stares at her. I pull my hand from his, and his eyes quickly look down at them before he looks back at her.

I'm not sure how to react. I don't know what to do. I wait for something—*anything*—to happen to let me know that my whole world as I know it here isn't about to come crashing down around me. For him to make a comment about how he had no idea he had a child. For him to say he's the wrong guy. *Anything.* But he just looks at her.

"How...how did you find me?" he whispers to her.

Oh, God.

It's true.

He has a daughter.

And he *knew* he did.

I see the tears welling in her eyes, and then I look at him. And they're welling in his eyes, too. And suddenly, I'm seeing in tunnel vision. I back up from them slowly, then a little quicker. He calls after me, taking a step in my direction, but I see him being torn apart.

I see him having to choose.

And he can't choose me.

Once I'm around the corner, I start running. The cottage is four miles outside of town, but I don't have another plan right now. I make my way down Main Street before I slow down to a walk, the freezing air burning in my throat.

I sniff in a few times, trying desperately to at least make it out of town before the tears come. I make it to the coffee shop, but that's as far as they'll let me get. Just as I'm reaching the edge of downtown, I hear someone call out my name.

"Where you off to in this weather, hon?" I hear Mickey say. I try to force a smile, but as he gets closer, his eyes fill with worry. He puts an arm around my shoulder and pulls me toward him. "Come on, hon. I'll take you home."

I don't fight him. I just thank the heavens that I didn't have to choose between walking in the freezing cold for miles or choosing to ride with Cash right now. My phone rings off the hook in my purse, and I know it's him, but I don't even look at it. I just buckle up in the front seat of Mickey's station wagon and wait to get home. He pulls into the drive, and I point out which cottage is mine. He parks the car and puts his hand on mine.

"Give it time, hon," he says with a forced smile. "Whatever it is, just give it time."

I nod and thank him for the ride. Then, I go inside, close and lock the door, and walk toward the fireplace. I reach into my purse and turn my phone off. Then, I sink to the floor in front of the couch, and I cry.

CHAPTER FOURTEEN

cash

I'M PULLING up to the cottage about two hours after I last saw her. My stomach is in knots, my hands are clammy, and my head is pounding.

I haven't felt this nervous in a very long time.

This unsettled.

When I realized Stevie was gone, I had asked Eden for her number. I told her that I just wanted to make sure my friend got home, and that I would call her and wanted to meet up with her. She seemed to be okay with it, but when I took off down the street to look for her, Mickey's son told me he had taken her home. I must have called her a thousand times by now, but she hasn't answered.

So, I went back to where I left Eden, and we talked for a few minutes. She had heard from someone local that I had been looking for her. That I had been asking around town about her for the last three years. And she wanted to see for herself if it was true. She'd asked around about me, and one of the locals pointed out my truck. So, she waited.

I know I need to make sure Stevie is okay.

I know I need to sit down with my...my *daughter*.

God, that feels so insane to say.

But right now, I just need a moment to process the last hour of my life.

I have a *child*.

She's big and grown and beautiful. She looks so much like her mother, especially at that age. But she's got my eyes—almost the same deep blue—and my brown hair. Kaydee was blonde, but other than that, Eden has almost all of her features.

I can't believe she's mine.

So many things are running through me right now. Pure joy at the thought of finally finding her—or of her finding *me*. Anger, at both myself and Kaydee for what we did, the lives we led that brought us to this moment, to me never having met my own child until she was twenty-two years old. Confusion about what my life is supposed to look like next. If she will want a real relationship with me. Where that will take me.

And then, I lift my eyes and look at the little cottage that sits on the water where I've spent some of the happiest moments of my entire life over the last few months.

And that's when the heartbreak sets in. Because I know I've scared her. I know I'll scare her some more. I know I have to come clean about my past. And I know it could mean the end for us.

All I've ever wanted since the day I laid eyes on her, since the moment I knew about what she'd been through, was to let her know that to me, she would be first. She became my world in a short amount of time. Now, I need to be a fucking man and walk in there and have a conversation with her. Now, I have to walk in there and tell her that I no longer know if that's the truth.

I draw in a deep, sharp breath, open my truck door, and get out. I knock on the door but don't hear anything. I think about pulling out my key, but it feels wrong to use it right now. She made it clear she wanted space. If we're going to talk, it has to be on her terms. I peek through the window and see the only light coming from the living room. I walk around to the side of the house and look through the porch windows, and my heart splinters.

She's sitting on the ground, a blanket draped over her shoulders. Tears stream down her face, and she presses her knuckles to her lips as she cries. I know I should probably sneak away, pretend I didn't see her like this.

But I can't. It goes against my every instinct.

She needs to be fixed. Even if I'm the one that broke her. I open the screen porch door and walk across the planks, tapping lightly on the glass door. She jumps, then our eyes meet. She stands slowly and walks toward the door, swiping at her tears before she unlocks it. She turns away as I walk inside, taking her seat on the floor once again. I freeze at first, watching her. Then, I walk toward her and sit down in front of her. I reach out and put my hand on hers. She flinches, but I don't let her move it.

"Look at me," I beg her. Slowly, she does. "I need to tell you some things, but I need you to stay with me while I do. Okay?"

She lets out a long breath, then nods slowly. Finally, her big blue eyes lift to mine.

I feel myself get shaky. I haven't told anyone this story in a very long time. I made peace with who I was and what I've done. But not everyone else has. I'm used to the disappointment so many people in my life felt toward me. But I so desperately do not want to feel that from Stevie.

You have no choice. Tell her.

"When I was a kid, I didn't have the most involved parents. My dad left when I was nine, and my mom worked odd jobs to keep food on the table. She met this guy, Gus, who had money. Turned out, he had money because he was one of the biggest drug dealers on Long Island. It didn't take long for my mom to get hooked— both on him and the drugs."

I watch as her eyes widen, but she doesn't move. She just stares at me, waiting. I swallow.

"They were on again, off again for most of my high school years. It was completely toxic, and she couldn't let him go because he was her dealer *and* her boyfriend. So, I spent most of my junior and senior year with my girlfriend, Kaydee. Kaydee was the only saving grace I had."

seventeen years ago

CHAPTER FIFTEEN

cash

SEVENTEEN YEARS EARLIER

"And the Tymesville Tigers have won!" the announcer calls over the loudspeaker as the bleachers erupt into a massive cheer. Kaydee is jumping up and down, and I see her brown curls bobbing up and down under her beanie. She is so freakin' beautiful. I get emotional sometimes, just looking at her. My friends don't get it. They think I'm whipped, that we spend too much time together. But I really don't give a shit.

Kaydee has given me so much more than a little teenage relationship. She's given me so much more than sex or lust or first experiences. She's given me stability. A literal place to lay my head when my mom is off her fucking rocker. When her dumbass boyfriend puts his hands on me with a little too much pressure. She's given me family—*her* family—and they've let me into their home with open arms.

I have a reputation around town. I'm the tweaker's son. The crackhead's spawn. I know it. I know how people see me. I know why people in town won't hire me for odd jobs, or why I don't get invited to a lot of parties.

But the Hamilton family? They don't care about any of that. They never once looked at me differently. They let me in the second they knew their daughter loved me. I've had to go to church with them a few times, but it's a small price to pay for the comfort they bring me. Family dinners with no TV trays or frozen meals. Laughter and jokes instead of drugs and screaming.

They don't have a big house. They don't make a ton of money.

They just have each other. They have happiness.

And they've let me in on it. Kaydee has let me in on it.

And I won't forget how lucky I am.

Every time I look at her, I know how fucking lucky I am. That she saw through the bullshit to who I am, in spite of my mother. In spite of my last name. And they did, too.

And tonight, we are going back to her house to celebrate the win. We will probably watch a movie with her parents. We will probably fool around on the couch once they go up to bed. And then, I'll sleep in their guest room and wake up to Mrs. Hamilton's pancakes.

"You ready?" I ask her, and she nods, taking my hand as I bend down to kiss her forehead.

"Sure am," she says, pulling her keys out of her coat pocket. Another thing I'm grateful for—transportation. Her little fifteen-year-old sedan has become like a magic carpet for me, carrying me to safety.

And every time I watch her drive away in it, I think to myself that one day, I'll buy her a bigger, newer car. Maybe one she'll drive our kids around in. Kaydee makes me want to be better. To *do* better. I want a family like hers. I want *her* to be my family. I want her to be proud to have my name. Not because of my family, but because it's *mine*.

"Can we stop by my house really fast? I just need to run in and grab some clothes," I ask her. She smiles and presses up to her tiptoes so she can kiss me. I'm a full foot taller than her, so I bend down to give her some help.

"Sure," she says.

She's been with me to my house a handful of times. I try hard to make it so that whenever we go, it's mid-afternoon so that it will be right around when my mom is either going into work or already gone. That's the time she's least likely to be completely fucked up. So far, I've succeeded. Although, it hasn't protected Kaydee from seeing how it fucks with me when I see her like that. Hasn't stopped her from holding me or rubbing my head so I can fall asleep when I talk about it.

She's been an angel in my life this last year. And maybe we're only seventeen, but I don't take it lightly.

We pull up to my house about ten minutes later, and when I see my mom's and Troy's cars in the driveway, I tell her to wait outside.

"I'll be out in a minute," I tell her, swallowing nervously as I jog up the front walk and into the house. As soon as I do, the air changes. The smell of smoke lingers in the air, but it's more than that. There's something thicker in it.

"Mom?" I call. But there's no response. The living room television is blaring, and I switch it off. "Mom?" I call again as I climb the stairs. And then I open her bedroom door, and that's when I see her. *Them.*

He's sitting against the headboard in the bed, hunched over, one eye closed, one partially open. The band is still around his arm, and the needle is sticking out of his skin.

And there she sits. My mother. On the floor like a piece of trash. Keeled over on the ground, the needle still sticking out of her arm.

Her skin is this weird, purple-grayish color. Her hair is disheveled, covering half her face. And then, I can't move. I can't breathe. I can't speak. I drop to my knees on the ground and crawl toward her slowly, my throat feeling like it's closing with every inch I close between us.

How dare she do this? How dare she fucking do this? How dare she make me hate her while I still love her? And then have the nerve to leave me like *this*?

Just as I reach her, I hear a blood-curdling scream, and I see Kaydee behind me in the doorway. And then, she's shaking and covering her mouth. I want to run to her, shield her from this, but the truth is, I'm so frozen from it, so numb, that I can't. She shakily reaches into her pocket and pulls out her phone, and I hear her making the 911 call.

And then, a lot of shit starts to happen.

We hear the sirens first, then see the lights. They

get upstairs, and a nice EMT moves me out of the way while I watch them give my mom NarCan and take her vitals. Two more EMTs are doing chest compressions on Troy. Kaydee is clutching onto me, both of us on the ground, and she holds my head to her chest. Through all the trauma I've just put her through, she's still trying to shield *me*.

You don't deserve her.

I know it's true. I've always known on some level that it's true.

I know it now like I knew it then. But right now, I can't afford to lose her. I need her too much.

I hear one of the EMTs pronounce Troy dead.

And then a moment later, I hear another one say they have a pulse on my mom.

They lift her onto a gurney and take her out of the room.

A police officer kneels down in front of us and asks if I have anywhere to stay tonight.

Kaydee tells them she's called her parents and that I can stay with them.

The next thing I know, I'm climbing into the back of their van as Mrs. Hamilton reaches her hand back to hold mine.

We get to their house, and she's making me a cup of hot tea at the table. Kaydee sits next to me, her hand on my thigh. Mrs. Hamilton sits on my other side, rubbing my back and stirring the cup in front of me. Mr. Hamilton sits across from me.

"We're here for you, honey," she says. "And you are welcome to stay here as long as you need to."

"Absolutely," Mr. Hamilton says. "We are here for whatever you need." I nod and thank them both, and they say goodnight and go up to bed.

You don't deserve them.

Kaydee asks if I want to go watch TV to take my mind off things. But I shake my head and tell her I'm pretty tired. She nods and walks me to the living room, fluffing my pillow and pulling my blanket back. I lie down, and she kneels beside the couch, pushing my hair back from my face and kissing my cheek, then my nose, then my other cheek. She pulls my face to hers so our foreheads touch.

"Oh, my sweet boy," she whispers, a small sob escaping her mouth. "I'm so sorry. I love you so much."

I don't say anything. I just feel the tears streaming down my face and into her hair.

"I'm here, okay?" she whispers. "I'm right here."

You don't deserve her.

I don't know what to say. I can't say anything. I just sit here for a moment, thinking about all the darkness I've just brought to this family. To Kaydee.

I say goodnight to her and lie back on the couch, with the stove light the only brightness in the room. She goes upstairs, and I lie still for a few minutes, listening to the grandfather clock in the corner of the room tick and tock. It normally soothes me. But tonight, it seems to be matching up with my quickening pulse and the beads of sweat dripping from my forehead.

Tonight, it feels like it's making my heart beat so hard that it feels like it might explode.

And then, suddenly, I can't be here anymore. I sit up and slide my shoes on. I walk toward the front door and lift her keys from the key ring. I open the door quietly and close it behind me.

And then, I take Kaydee's car, and I drive back to my empty house.

I walk up the stairs to my mother's room.

I kneel down on the carpet where I found her. Where I thought I'd lost her. And maybe, I did.

And then, I scream out.

I scream her name. I pound my fists to the floor. The tears and spit spew from me as I curse my mother for being who she is. For being someone who can break me the way she has. When I calm myself down, I sit back against the wall.

And then, I see something that catches my eye.

Underneath the bed is a needle and a syringe.

Untouched.

Maybe this was a hiding spot.

Maybe it fell off the nightstand.

I don't know.

But I think of the way my mother looked when she lay there on this ground. Numb. Peaceful.

I think of the way Kaydee held me, sat with me through all the darkness until she could pull me back into the light.

You don't deserve her.

I don't.

I don't deserve to get to attach her to this. To get to pull her into the darkness that is this house. The darkness that runs through my veins because of who birthed me.

She should be free from this.

From me.

I grab the band from the ground that was tightened around my mother's arm just a few hours earlier. And then, I pick up the needle. I flick it like I've seen her do a few times when she didn't know I was watching. And then, I straighten my arm, and I press it to my skin. And just as I'm about to push it in, I hear her.

"Stop," she whimpers, and I see Kaydee standing in my mother's doorway again, her lip trembling. She rushes toward me, putting her hand on top of the syringe and staring straight into my eyes.

But I can't bear it, so I look away.

You're a fucking coward. You. Don't. Deserve. Her.

"Please, don't do this," she cries. "You are better than this. You are better than her."

I cry as I look up at her, the tears just streaming now. I'm not sobbing, but they're just flowing on their own, like I have no control.

"I'm not," I tell her. "I'm not! I'm not better than this. I'm not better than her. You are. *You* are better than this. And you should go."

Her eyes widen as she jolts back.

Her chest heaves up and down. And then, she reaches her hand out and takes the syringe from my arm.

"But I'm not better without *you*," she says, the tears dropping from her chin to the floor. She stands up and moves back across the room. I make a move toward her, but she holds out one hand. Then, she puts the needle to her own arm, and before I can say anything, she presses it into her skin.

"No!" I scream. "What are you doing?"

"If you're going, then you're taking me with you," she says and then empties it into her arm. She stumbles around for a moment, and then I grab her, pulling the needle out of her arm and carrying her into my room. I lay her down on the bed. I try desperately to think of the things Troy and my mom would do for each other when they were too strung out. I prop her up on my pillow and grab some water for when she comes down. And then, I go into my mom's room and search desperately through her shit. I find another needle and a bag of heroin. I grab the spoon and lighter she keeps in her nightstand drawer, and I light it up. And in a few moments time, I'm lying next to Kaydee in my bed, letting the heroin soak into my blood and take over my body.

Because if I have taken her down, she's sure as hell not going down alone.

And as I seep into the black, the last thought I have is that I've ruined her.

You don't deserve her.

present day

CHAPTER SIXTEEN

cash

☀

I PAUSE FOR A MOMENT, taking a breath and trying to gauge where Stevie is. If she's processing, if she's judging, if she's planning her escape. But I've got nothing. I have absolutely no idea where her head is right now. She's just staring at me blankly, her eyes filled with tears that haven't fallen. She just keeps her eyes on me, so I go on. Now, I'm getting to the real meat of the story. The part where I confess how awful of a human I am. About how I got my high school girl-friend hooked on heroin.

My high school girlfriend who was top of our class. Who was a state-ranked swimmer.

"After that night, we got high together weekly. Whenever my mom was out, we'd sneak her shit. We slept through prom, almost didn't graduate. And then, one day, I woke up, and she was gone."

She's still sitting as still as a statue, staring like she doesn't know what to do or say. She's just looking, and

I'm desperate to know what she's thinking. But I can't stop here.

"I looked for her for months. Her entire family was gone. When I went to her house, it was empty. A man inside told me they had put it up for rent. She wouldn't answer my calls. She didn't come back to school. It was like she had vanished into thin air." I swallow back what feels like knives in my throat as my eyes drop to my hands. I pull a leg up and rest my elbow on it.

"A few months later, I ran into her neighbor at the grocery store and asked what happened. I'll never forget the look she gave me that day. She told me that they took her away to get clean."

I feel her eyes get wider, but I don't dare look at her —not if I want to finish this.

"She had gotten hooked because of me," I say, my voice cracking. She moves slightly so her foot touches mine. "So, they took her away. A clean break from me, the town, anything that might pull her back. It wasn't until a few years ago when my mom ran into someone else in town that told her it was also because she was pregnant. Until then, I had no idea. I still didn't. I searched everywhere, for her parents, her sister, her, but I hit dead ends everywhere. No social media, nothing. When we were younger, Kaydee had mentioned she loved summers in Blue Bay with her grandparents. This was the only place I hadn't looked, so I came. And until last night, I still had no luck. I was beginning to think there was no way it was true until she showed up at my truck last night. I'm so sorry that that's how it went down. I'm so sorry, Stevie."

I take one final breath and raise my eyes to hers.

Please understand.

She swallows again, wiping at her eyes.

"I'm…I'm sorry that all that happened to you," she says. "I'm sorry about your mom. And I don't want you to think that I think any differently of you because of your past, or the drugs, or any of it. Because I don't. You were a kid, and you had a lot missing. And I'm so, so sorry," she says. And then she crawls across the floor and throws her arms around my neck. She holds me tight for a moment, stroking the back of my hair. "You deserved better," she whispers. I let my arms slink around her middle, holding her tight, but more letting her hold me. She pulls apart from me, cupping my face in her hands. "You deserved better," she says again, her eyes welling with tears. And now, mine are, too. "What you did then doesn't have anything to do with who you are and what you are now, Cash. I need to know that you hear me." She looks at me and raises an eyebrow at me. I nod slowly. No one has ever said anything remotely close to this to me before.

Breathe. She's still here.

"I'm so sorry that you lost so much time with her," she says as she scoots back a bit from me. "It's unfair. And Kaydee had a whole family rooting for her, pulling her out of it. You did it on your own, and you should be so proud of yourself, Cash."

I nod, but I feel this weird haze descending on us as her eyes drop to the ground. She retreats further from me and crosses her arms over her chest.

Wait…

"Cash, you...you have become the person my sun rises and sets with over these last few months. It happened so fast that I didn't realize it *was* happening. But..."

Wait. No. Stop.

"I can't...I can't be a second choice. I'm sorry. I wish it didn't sound so selfish, but I can't take any more conditional love." She pushes herself to stand, and I stand with her. My whole body trembles.

You don't deserve her...

"You have to see where this goes with her. You owe it to her, and you owe it to yourself. And if you didn't take the time to try and make something of this, you wouldn't be the man I thought you were. I'm so sorry," she says, her bottom lip trembling. "But I can't wait to see if I fit into the picture. I have to start painting my own." She pulls me into her, leaving a long, soft kiss on my lips. And as she does, I taste the salt of her tears on my lips. "I'm sorry, Cash," she manages to get out. "But you have to go." Then, her hands drop from my cheeks, and she slips around me, making her way up the stairs.

This is what you deserve.

To be alone.

To lose everything.

To lose her.

stevie

IT'S A SURREAL FEELING, being in love.

Because at any given moment, you can be as high as you have ever, or will ever be.

And in the next, you can be lower than you ever thought was possible. To the point where you're not even sure if you exist.

It's been two days, and I haven't heard from him. I'm not sure what I'd expect him to say if he did call, though. There's not much he can say that can change anything. Because the fact is, he has a child that he didn't know about. He has twenty years to make up for. He has arguably the most important relationship in his life to account for. To establish. To try and nurture before it's too late.

Nothing can change that. And nothing should. Not even me.

If things were different, if *I* were different, maybe I'd tell him I'd wait for him. Maybe I'd be more casual, letting him do what he needed to do. Maybe I'd wait.

But the truth is, I'm tired. I'm so tired of waiting to be enough for someone. I'd rather be enough for myself than wait around and see if I ever amount to it for someone else. I've been down that road, and I'm the one who ends up getting burned in the end.

I can't, and I won't do it again.

In a cruel trick of the universe, I picture Cade. And not just Cade. Cade *and* Tess. The woman the universe picked out for him, and the one that it carved the most crooked, criss-crossed, fucked-up path to. A path that ran me right the fuck over.

But still, she was his, and he was hers. Even when he was mine.

And as I lie alone in this bed, the waves crashing beneath my window outside, all I can think about is that I want to be someone's Tess. I want to be the person that stops someone's Earth on its axis.

I want the breath to run away from someone's body when they see me coming.

The way the breath ran away from me when I heard his truck park in the driveway here in Blue Bay. The way my entire body reacted anytime Cash touched me. The way I couldn't fathom a night without him after just two months.

But here I am, alone in this bed, sleeping without him.

A few more days pass, and my phone has rung twice. Once was my boss, letting me know that a conference call we were supposed to have was being postponed. The other was Della, checking to see if I was alive. I still haven't brought myself to give her the whole story. All she knows is that it's over and that I'm in the reeling phase. I need my time. I check it every hour or so, just to see if he's called or texted. And then, I want to kick myself every time when I realize he hasn't.

I let my mind wander every now and then, wondering where he is, what he's doing. If he and Eden have met up. If they've talked. Then, it gets dangerous. Because then I *want* to know. I want to make sure he's okay. That he's not faulting himself for missing out on her. That he's showing himself some grace. That he's letting go of the mistakes he made when he was seventeen.

The fucked-up thing is, if Eden weren't part of the equation, I'd be killing myself to make sure he knew all of that. That he can take responsibility without condemning himself to a life of misery and emptiness. That he can acknowledge his own shortcomings, the bad choices he made, but also acknowledge how far he's come. That despite it all, he did learn to show love. That he got it in return.

But now, he'll never know.

And that's what breaks me the most.

CHAPTER EIGHTEEN

I KNOW this feeling because I've done it so many times.

I'm auto-piloting.

I'm taking life one step at a time, pretending like there aren't asteroids falling around me. Pretending that the world as I know it isn't crumbling.

Pretending like the last months with her didn't happen.

Like I can survive without her.

I went to a therapist once after I left my mom's and finally got my shit together. She said that my tendency to avoid was a product of the trauma I'd been through. That was the only time I saw her. I didn't feel like it was fair to let someone tell me I'd been "through" something when I'd caused just as much of it myself.

So here I am, twenty years later, dealing with my shit in the same damn way. One thing I'm not avoiding, though, is the fact that I found my daughter—or rather, she found me. Despite everything with Stevie, the one thing that has been unwavering since I talked to her last was that I will not give up on Eden. I will not let her down. If she wants me in her life, she will have me.

And on that note, I put the truck in park at the cafe outside of town where she asked me to meet up today. I'm so nervous I feel like I'm going to throw up. I take in a deep breath, then slide out, locking up behind me. But just as I start to walk in the direction of the door, I stop when I hear someone call my name.

Someone who hasn't called my name in over twenty years.

Kaydee Hamilton.

The once-love of my life.

And as I have very recently learned, the mother of my child.

I freeze when I see her walking toward me.

She looks so much the same. A few more wrinkles around her eyes, but still as beautiful as ever. I feel this overwhelming sense of relief when I see her.

She's alive. She's okay. You didn't ruin her.

She stops a few feet away from me, and for a moment, we just stare at each other.

And then, she smiles, and I feel my stomach flip.

She's okay. She's happy.

"Kaydee," I whisper as she walks toward me, closer, until her arms are around me.

I can't hold it together when she hugs me. I'm so overwhelmed with emotion, swimming in relief that I didn't completely fuck her up for the rest of her life. After a moment, we come apart, and I hold her at arm's length, just looking her up and down.

"You look amazing," I tell her, and she smiles, tears in her eyes. She swipes the one streaming down my cheek and hugs me again. "What are you doing here?"

We come apart again, and she sniffs, shaking her head to clear out the emotion still left in her eyes. She draws in a long breath.

"Before you sat down with our daughter, I wanted to talk to you," she says. "And I wanted to make sure you were…" She pauses, biting her lip. I swallow and nod.

"Sober," I say with a slow nod. "It's okay. I would want to know that, too. But I am. Going on twenty years next month." She smiles and nods slowly, her eyes welling with tears again. "And you?"

"Going on twenty-three years in the fall," she says. I nod and squeeze her hand.

"Kaydee, I… I'm so… I'm so…" I want to say so much. I want to apologize. I want to tell her how glad I am that she became something, that she didn't let me drag her down with me. But I can't. And thank God she doesn't make me. She just pulls me in again. She rubs my back as she squeezes me.

"We were kids, Cash," she says. "We were just kids. It was all you knew, and all I knew was how to love you." We come apart again, and she cups my cheeks. "And you know what? I got the best damn thing out of it. That girl. She saved my life."

I nod, letting her words cascade over me. The reunion of the fucking century, shaking me to my core. And through all of it, there's this voice in the back of my mind.

145

I wish Stevie was here. I wish she could meet her.

We go into the cafe and grab a table by the window. She orders a hot tea, and I order a coffee, and then we peruse the menu slowly, ordering appetizers and barely touching them as we make up for twenty-plus years of lost time.

I learn that she's been married for almost ten years to a guy named Rob. He's the principal at their local high school, and he basically helped raise Eden. There's a knife that cuts through me when she talks about him, but not because he's with her. God knows, all I ever wanted for Kaydee since the last day I saw her was for her to be happy. To be loved the right way. And I can tell by the look in her eye when she talks about him, that she is.

But this guy, he came in and raised my child. The kid I didn't even know about. He walked into her life, and he raised her. I'm so glad he did. But I so badly wish I could have been there just to witness it, if nothing else.

The anguish of it must be visible on my face, because she pauses and rests her hand on mine from across the table.

"Cash," she says, then she pauses again, her eyes falling and her lip starting to tremble. "I'm...I'm so sorry. There were so many times I wanted to reach out to you. I wanted you to know about her. But I was so scared that...I was scared you hadn't gotten better. And it wasn't just about me and you anymore. It was only about her. But I look at you now, and I'm...I'm so *proud* of you, Cash. The handyman business? You getting your shit together completely alone? Do you know how impossible that is?"

I smile faintly, just looking down at our hands on the table.

"I'm so proud of you, Cash. But I'm also proud of the seventeen-year-old boy I used to love so much." I raise my eyes to her, brows knitted together. A tear streams down her face. "The man in front of me would have made him so damn proud," she whispers. "And I know he's going to make his daughter so proud, too."

I squeeze her hand and nod, letting it all soak in. A few more minutes pass, and she tells me about Eden being the valedictorian of her high school and getting into all five schools she applied to with flying colors. She tells me she's practical, but she's also an artist. She loves painting but has her sights set on a graphic design degree so she can get a good job. I smile.

My daughter.

I have a daughter.

"So, what about you?" she asks. "You told me about the handyman business, the houses," she says, "but what about *you?* What makes you happy these days, Cash?"

I freeze. I like fixing things up. I like seeing them come back to life with a good sanding, a new coat of paint, a stronger base.

But what makes me happy?

"Stevie," I say just above a whisper, a smile crossing my lips. She raises an eyebrow.

"As in…?" she asks, perplexed. I laugh.

"She's staying in one of the cottages I keep up," I say. Her eyebrows drop, and she nods.

"Ah, 'she.' I wasn't sure if maybe a lot more had changed over the last two decades than I realized," she says, and we both laugh. "Tell me about her. Are you...together?"

I take my time before answering.

"We were...I think," I say. "But the whole finding-out-you-have-a-kid thing kinda put a wrench in it."

Her eyes widen.

"Oh, Cash, I'm sorry," she says, but I hold up my hand.

"I knew there was a possibility that Eden existed," I say. "But I didn't tell her, and I should have."

She nods.

"Cash," she says, "I'm so glad that you and Eden are going to have this time together. I know there's a lot to make up for, and I want nothing more than for her to have a relationship with you. But if Stevie is it, if she's what makes you happy, you can't let her go, either. You owe it to your seventeen-year-old self to live the best life you possibly can. Let yourself feel the love that he never did."

My eyes lift to hers, and I smile.

Before I can say anything else, someone appears next to me, and when I look up, I see that it's my daughter.

"Well, this is...weird," she says, and all three of us laugh. She looks at Kaydee. "Did you make sure he's not a junkie yet?"

Kaydee shoots her a look, then looks back at me, cheeks flushed. I chuckle and shake my head.

"I'm sorry," she says. "She's a bit of a smartass, this one." Then, she slides from the booth and turns to our daughter, kissing her on the forehead.

"I'm just saying... I've missed out on some time with him," Eden says, sliding into the booth where her mother was sitting. "I'd like to catch up now." She takes her mother's hand and winks, kissing it before Kaydee brushes her hair.

"Don't miss another minute on my account," she says. Then, she looks up at me. "Have a good time. She's a lot like you, so be careful."

Then, she walks out the door, and I'm sitting alone at a table with my daughter.

She juts a thumb back in Kaydee's direction.

"Isn't she still such a babe?" she asks. I laugh and nod, taking a sip of my coffee.

"Always was," I say. "I'm not surprised in the least."

There's a short pause, then she taps her hands on the table.

"Before we start," she says, "you should know a few things about me. I get hangry real

easily, and I'm dangerously close to approaching hunger. Second, awkward silences make me very uncomfortable, so we have to just keep talking, okay?"

I smile and nod, waving toward our waitress.

"Hi, can we get another order of fries, some mozzarella sticks, and a stack of onion rings?" The waitress looks at me, eyebrows raised, like she's trying to see if I'm kidding or not. I smile. "We have a lot of catching up to do." She nods and turns away, and l look back at Eden.

"That'll work," she says. "Excellent choice with the fried food."

I laugh.

"Does your mom still eat like a rabbit?" I ask. She nods.

"Ugh. *Yes*," she says.

"Well, then don't tell her about this," I laugh. She smiles back at me. Before there can be a moment of quiet, I lean back in my chair. "So, Eden, give me the highlights."

She raises an eyebrow as she takes a sip of the Coke in front of her.

"The highlights?" she asks.

"Yep." I nod. "Give me the highlights of your life so far. The good, the bad, the ugly. Like you're telling someone your life story—because you kind of are."

She smiles and nods, taking another sip and plucking a fry off the plate that the waitress has just set in front of her. She rests back against the booth, settling in. And then, she starts to tell me. She tells me about how they lived with Kaydee's parents until she was five, when Kaydee finally finished her degree and was able to afford an apartment outside of Boston. She met Rob when Eden was seven, and they dated for years before he proposed. Rob was good to her and never treated her like she wasn't his.

She played lacrosse in high school and was MVP her junior and senior year. She got a few division II offers to play but decided she wanted to focus on her classes and making friends. She double-majored in art and graphic design, so she has one extra semester to go. It's finishing up strong, and she's back to focusing on friends.

"And girls," she says. "I wanted to focus on girls." She takes a sip of her Coke, one eyebrow raised, waiting for my reaction. But I don't give her much of one. I just met her. I am still getting used to the fact that I *have* a child. I don't give a rat's ass who she's interested in—as long as they treat her right. I just nod and smile, taking a sip of my drink, too.

"And? Did you find any?" I ask.

She smiles.

"I dated this girl from New York last semester," she says, "but she was a little bit bougie for me. We're taking a break for now."

I nod.

"The right girl will come along," I tell her. "Don't rush it."

"Has the right girl come along for you?" she asks matter-of-factly, and our eyes catch.

I nod.

"Ya know, Eden, I think she has," I tell her, my eyes falling to my hand on the table as I swirl my fork around.

"Was it the girl I saw you with by your truck?" she asks. I nod.

"That was her," I tell her.

"You need to fix whatever happened, okay?" she says, and my eyes find hers again.

"How do you know something needs fixing?" I ask. She shrugs.

"I could see it in your eyes, the second she came up just now," she says. "That's not a face that says, 'All is well.'"

I chuckle.

"This is just the face that God gave me," I say, motioning to it.

She laughs and points to her own.

"I know. Because it's the same one he gave me," she says. "Mom always used to say I had your puppy-dog eyes."

I laugh and look at her.

"You kind of do," I tell her. She nods and smiles.

"I see that now," she says.

We talk a little longer, laughing at each other's stories, nodding and listening intently to the darker stuff. She doesn't ask much about my family, thank God, and I imagine it's because Kaydee already filled her in. But I make a vow, right here at this table, that I will never hide anything from this girl. Whatever pieces of me she wants to know about, she will. Finally, we both agree to call it a night, and I pay the bill.

We stand to leave, and I follow her out the door.

I turn to her, but before I can figure out what to say next, she speaks.

"Do you want to be in my life, Cash?" she asks.

I look down at her, her brown locks dancing in the breeze. I nod.

"I do," I say. She nods, then she sticks a hand out.

"Welcome," she says with a smile. Then, before I

know it, she throws her arms around my neck and hugs me. I wrap my arms around her, and for the first time in my life, I know what it feels like to hold a piece of your heart in your hands. I set her back down, and she looks up at me. "There's always been a place for you," she says, putting a hand on her chest. "I'm just glad it can be filled now." I smile at her, holding back the tears I'm feeling.

"Me, too," I tell her.

We say our goodbyes and a promise to stay in close touch. She goes back to Boston tomorrow and then won't have much free time till she graduates. I'm filled with so much warmth and fear that I don't know what to do next.

All I know is, I want to tell Stevie.

And I want to tell her now.

A few minutes later, I'm pulling up to the cottage. I'm on such a high—both from having sat down with my own flesh and blood, but also the adrenaline of making a relationship with her work—that I don't notice the empty driveway at first.

And then, I walk up to the front door, and I don't see her things on the counter through the windows.

Her mug isn't on the counter, with old coffee sticking to the sides of it.

Her slippers aren't on the floor next to the door. Her yoga mat isn't rolled up next to the fireplace.

No part of her is here.

She's gone.

CHAPTER NINETEEN

stevie

"ONE, TWO, *THREE!*" I call out to Jax as I run toward him in Della's backyard. He squeals like a pig as he runs around, climbing up his swing set and ducking into the corner of his pirate ship. He pushes his face between two of the bars, then sticks his tongue out at me. "Oh, that's it!" I say, running up the slide and grabbing him. We fall to the wood in a fit of laughter as I tickle his sides. I love this boy. Cade and I moved to town right around the time he was born. Della and I met at a party one night and hit it off right away. Her husband died while she was pregnant with Jax, and although it has to be one of the hardest things someone can go through, I've had the pleasure to watch her blossom into the best mother I know. This kid has no idea how lucky he is.

"Okay, you two," she calls from the house, "lunch is ready!"

We go down the slide together, him giggling all the way. I've gotten to watch this little boy grow into the precocious little boy he is, and I am so grateful. I've been staying with them for the last two days since I got back to Maryland. I couldn't stay in that cottage. The place that had given me so much freedom, that had let me breathe, had suddenly become the place that was suffocating me. I haven't told anyone else I'm here. I don't want the drama of my mom. I don't want my coworkers asking to meet up for happy hour.

I just need time.

Again.

I'm so sick of needing time.

We eat our sandwiches and fruit out on the patio while Jax takes three bites and takes to playing again. I watch him with a smile, picking at my grapes, still not able to eat a full meal. Della takes another sip of her lemonade, then puts her glass down on the table and clears her throat to get my attention. My eyes snap to her.

"Can I just say something?" she says. I take a slow sip of my lemonade, waiting for the blow. "You are more miserable to be around now than you were after the divorce."

I choke on my drink, a mix of laughter and being appalled.

I shake my head as I clear my throat, putting my glass back down on the table.

"Um, thanks?" I say with a smile. Della is not delicate. But she's the perfect type of friend for me. She's exactly what I need. She's real all the time.

"I don't mean that in a bitchy way. I really don't. I mean, maybe a little," she says with a smirk, and I laugh and roll my eyes. But then, her face gets serious, and she leans forward and covers my hand with hers. "After Cade, you were in shambles. Don't get me wrong. I watched you try and make sense of your life without him. But you weren't *lost,* ya know? You kept moving. But *this...*" she says, "*this* is way deeper than anything I've ever seen you feel. I know what it's like to lose the absolute love of your life, Stevie. Probably better than anyone." I look up at her, her eyes glassed over. I still remember Jackson's funeral, the way she looked in that black dress, her little baby bump popping out. I squeeze her hand. "Is that what this is, Steve?" she whispers. "Did you just lose the love of your life?"

I feel that burn in the back of my throat—the one I can only seem to fend off by distracting myself with Jax or watching trash TV with Della at night. I can't seem to bring myself to speak. I look down at my wrist, at the little string bracelet he gave me at the lighthouse the night he held me on that blanket on the ground.

The one I can't bring myself to take off. It's the last piece of him that I have.

I feel the tears burning at my eyes, and I shake my head and smile, pushing myself to stand.

"Don't make me say it, Dell," I whisper as I pat her hand and walk past her into the house.

I'm lying in Della's guest bed, staring up at the fan as it swirls around and around. Bedtime is the worst.

Almost as bad as trying to eat. I can't close my eyes because all I see is him. When I lie in bed, I start to smell him, like he's coming out of my pores.

So, I just lie, and stare, hoping that sleep comes before the sinking feeling of complete hopelessness.

I trudge down the steps the next morning in my cami and pajama shorts, my robe fluttering at my sides. Jax is already at the kitchen island, eating his cereal and watching cartoons while Della makes her protein shake.

"Morning," she calls to me over the sound of the blender before she shuts it off and jostles it around. She pours it into two cups and slides one toward me. "Drink," she demands. "You're wasting away."

I scoff as I begrudgingly take the cup.

"It's been three days," I say with an eye roll.

"Don't care," she says. "I won't have it on my watch."

I sip on my smoothie while she rushes Jax around, getting him dressed for school and making sure his lunch is packed. We walk him to the front door like we have for the last two days, kiss him goodbye, and wave as he runs out to the bus. We're standing on the porch of her little bungalow, and I watch as my source of happiness for the last few days drives off.

"Come on, kid," she says with a nudge. "You got the rest of your life to start living."

But as we turn to go back in the house, we both

turn back around when the rumble of a truck pulls up outside the house. And then, my whole heart drops to the ground. My stomach flips. My palms clam up, and I can't breathe.

He gets out and walks around, freezing when our eyes lock.

"Is…is that…?" Della says with a gasp.

I don't answer her. We both just stand still, frozen, while my mind tries to wrap around the fact that I'm seeing him here in Dalesville.

No one says anything for a minute, but leave it to Della not to let a moment of silence last too long.

"I'm Della," she says with a quick hand wave.

"Cash," he says, waving back, taking a few more steps up the front walk. "Permission to approach?"

She nods and smiles.

Damn him and his charm.

I pull my robe around myself a little tighter.

"How…how did you find me?" I ask as he gets to the steps.

"Well, uh, I went to Rie's. Ran into your ex while I was there…that was awkward. Although, he seems like a nice enough guy."

I swallow.

Dear God.

"Can we talk?" he asks, swallowing nervously as he looks up at me. God, I missed his face. His hair is a little messier than normal, and his face has a little stubble on it. He looks tired, probably from driving all the way down here. But I can't shake the feeling of relief just seeing him live and in the flesh.

I nod, and Della puts her hand on my shoulder.

"I'm gonna go inside," she says. "And I will most definitely not be pressing my ear to the door or staring out the window."

I smile faintly as she walks back inside and closes the door. I stand still, afraid to move, as he walks up the steps toward me.

I sit down on the top one, and he does the same.

"How…how did it go with…" I start, but he shakes his head and puts his hand on mine.

"Let me go first, okay?" he says. I nod, wrapping my arms around my middle.

"Yesterday, I met my daughter. My child. And… she's incredible, Steve. She really is. And I'm enamored and amazed and furious that I've missed so much time with her all at the same time. And the first thing I wanted to do when I left her was run to you and tell you about it." I swallow hard, already feeling my eyes start to burn. The truth is, I've been dying to know how it went. What she was like. What she thought of him. What he told her. I let him go on. "She goes back to school this week, and she's living in Boston. Boston is almost four hours from Blue Bay. She won't be able to come visit a lot, and I just…I don't want to miss more time with her, Steve. I don't. I want all the time with her I can get." I nod. As much as it guts me, I understand. And this is exactly how I'd want him to react in this situation. He wouldn't be the man I fell in love with if he didn't. So, I prepare myself. This is it. The rest of the Band-aid is coming off.

Let him crush you, Stevie. Then, it's time to heal.

I nod, refusing to let the tears fall.

"That's exactly what you should do," I tell him, trying to sound matter-of-fact. Emotionless. Like I'm not having the air sucked out of my lungs by his very presence, like my heart isn't being squeezed to death by every word he says. "She shouldn't have to go any longer not knowing her dad—especially when her dad is you," I tell him. Then, I force myself to look him in the eye. "And you deserve to know your daughter. You deserve good, Cash."

He has to know that I want this for him. Watching him drive away, watching him leave me behind, that'll be the death of me. But I love him too much to let my own selfish desires get in the way of what he deserves. Because the truth is, he deserves every single good thing that comes his way. And then some. He deserves it all. He thinks he's bad. He thinks he should be paying his penance for the rest of his life.

And the truth is, those of us who are lucky enough to have him in our lives, even if it's just for a moment, are lucky enough.

I know I am.

He stares at me, his deep blues boring into me like they're drilling holes.

"I've never been loved by anyone the way you love me, Stevie," he says. "Loved," he corrects himself. I stare at him. He takes my hand in both of his, lifting it to his lips. He kisses each knuckle gently. He lifts his eyes to mine. "I once told you I wanted to do something good with my life. To know that when I leave this Earth, I'll leave something worth a damn. But the truth is, you are what makes it all worth it. Even this next step. Maybe it's selfish of me, but you make me the best version of myself I've ever been. You make me *want* to be better. This journey I'm about to take with Eden, for instance. I need you with me. I know it's selfish of me, Steve. I know it's not the life you wanted. I know it's actually the exact fucking opposite of it." I smile faintly. "But I promise you that if you take it with me, I'll make it the life you want. I'll spend the rest of my days making yours good. I don't care if you're Stevie Sunshine, or Grumpy Stevie, or something in the middle. Just be *my* Stevie."

My eyes burn with tears, and then I can't stop them anymore. They stream down my cheeks like a fucking river, my lips trembling as they fall off the edges. He scoots closer to me, taking my face in his hand. His fingers start to swipe at them as he presses his lips to my forehead.

"Oh, my girl," he whispers, "don't let me cause you more tears. Just let me love you. Please." He holds his head to mine as I clutch onto his wrists. "I don't know where I'll be in a year. Five years. Fifty years," he says. "But if you're not with me, it's all pointless."

I force my eyes open and look at him.

I'm so scared. God, I'm scared. I've had my husband get diagnosed with cancer. I've had him leave me for the woman he said was his real soulmate. I've had a mother who used me my whole life.

I think about what he said a few moments ago.

I've never been loved the way you love me.

I've never been loved like this, either. I've never had

someone who wanted to let me have my own journey, but someone who wanted me to be a part of his so badly. Someone who didn't consider their life complete without me in it.

And the truth is, it would be the same way with me. I'm old enough to know that not every love will feel like this. In fact, I don't think anything else will ever feel like this ever again. I nod and smile.

"I'll follow you anywhere," I whisper through my tears. He smiles through his own glassy eyes, and I feel an instant release as he presses his lips to mine.

"Stick with me, woman," he says. "I'm all yours."

CHAPTER TWENTY

WE SPENT what felt like a second but was actually a full hour sitting on that porch, smiling, laughing, kissing like teenagers. She took me inside eventually and formally introduced me to Della who said that she was glad I came to my senses and that I was better looking than she thought I'd be. I could tell right away that we were going to be fast friends. I think she loves Stevie almost as much as I do.

Almost.

But now, as we sit at Della's kitchen table, drinking wine and laughing, I'm watching Stevie smile. And I know that no one on this Earth loves her as much as I do. No one ever will. I once thought I didn't deserve her. And maybe that's still true. But I know that I want to be a man that does. And with her, I will become him.

She called into work today, and so did Della. We waited for her adorable-as-hell son to get off his bus so I could meet him, played in the backyard for a little bit, and now, Stevie's looking up at me, her eyes big, glowing. I know that look.

"I need to find somewhere to stay tonight," I tell her. She gives me a look, her eyebrows knitting together.

"You're staying with me, you idiot," she says, her bottom lip sticking out a little bit. A fire lights low in my belly, and my dick twitches in my pants. God, no one can make my whole body come alive like she can. I fake salute.

"Yes, ma'am," I tell her. "I didn't drive ten hours to profess my love to you and then sleep without you. You're not getting rid of me."

She smiles, and I melt. I pull her closer to me as we watch Della push Jax on his swing. I lower my lips to her ear.

"But we're not staying here," I whisper. She looks up at me, one eyebrow raised.

"Where are we staying?" she asks.

I smile and shrug.

"Don't know. But like I said, I didn't drive ten hours to profess my love to you and sleep without you. But before we sleep, there are a lot of other things I need to do to you first."

She giggles as I pull her into me and nuzzle her neck. She kisses me and hops to her feet.

"I'll go pack my stuff."

She scurries away, and I tap her ass before she disappears into the house. Jax is running around the yard with a toy airplane, and Della is making her way up the porch steps. She sits down next to me and lets out a breath.

"God, that kid is gonna run me ragged," she laughs, "but I love it so much."

I laugh and look over at him.

"Endless energy, it seems," I say. She nods.

"Hmm, for damn sure," she says. "But it's worth it." Then, she looks over at me. "All of it. Even if you're late to the game." She winks at me.

"Ah," I say, "I take it you know my whole life story by now."

She laughs.

"Everything she knows, I probably know," she says. She pats my hand. "Whether you know them from the moment they're born, or from the time they turn twenty, it's a love like no other. And I know your whole life is about to change for the better. Congratulations," she says. I smile.

"Thanks, Della."

"This is where I would normally throw in the whole 'if you hurt her, I'll kill you' thing, but I get the feeling it's not needed here. So, I won't say it, but just don't forget it. Because I will."

I laugh and hold my hands up.

"Noted," I say. Then, her face gets a little more serious.

"Listen," she says, "Stevie is a person who always, *always* has it together. Always. She makes living look easy, one hundred percent of the time. This last year, she had the rug—the rug being life itself—pulled out from underneath her. She had no control over it. It all just happened to her. I've just been waiting for her to get it all back together, to grab hold of the reins again. But the beautiful thing is, she met you, and she didn't have to. Because you love her through it all. So, as her best friend, I just wanted to say, thank you. Thank you for holding her reins. Thank you for reminding her that it doesn't have to always rest on her."

I see a tear in her eye. I reach for her hand and pat it.

"She is my sunshine," I tell her. "Even on the dark days. She's my sunshine."

A few minutes later, we're saying our goodbyes and packing up my truck. We're leaving her car here, and then tomorrow, we will come back for it. We'll follow each other back to Blue Bay and figure out our next move from there.

But right now, I'm fucking starving.

"The salad was delicious," I tell her, "but I gotta get some real food before we call it a night."

She laughs.

"Let's hit Andy's on the way out of town," she says. "It's a few miles this way." She points, and I follow her direction.

Andy's is this little pizza place across from the fire-house in Dalesville. It's got a little bit of small-town charm, I guess, but honestly, I'm so hungry right now I could be sitting in a dumpster and be unbothered if someone put food in front of me. We sit down in a booth, and I rub her leg underneath it while we wait for our food and beer.

We eat and smile and laugh. She asks me a thousand questions about Eden—what she's like, what she's majoring in, if she's happy.

Questions a mother would ask.

I can't help but smile. I can't wait for them to meet.

I pay the bill, and we're out the door, in my truck, and on our way to the hotel a few minutes outside of town that she booked us a room in. And I cannot wait to get her in that room and get her naked. Kiss every inch of her body. Love her the way only I can.

A few minutes later, we're checking in, scurrying to the elevator, and making out like a bunch of kids. I'm rock hard before the elevator doors even shut, and my whole body feels like it's throbbing.

"Don't leave me again," I whisper in her ear between kisses. She nibbles on my neck and moans as my hand slides up the inside of her thigh, stopping at her center. "Hey," I say, letting my fingers dance along the crease of her jeans, "you hear me? Don't leave me again."

She nods as I start sliding my fingers back and forth, the friction building literally and figuratively.

"I won't leave," she mutters, still biting and sucking on my neck. The doors open, and I practically yank her off, taking her suitcase and rolling it out with the other hand. We get to our door, I unlock it, and throw our shit inside. Then, I grab her, pull her in, and slam the door, pushing her up against it. I kiss her ear, her neck, her shoulder.

"Tell me you're mine," I demand as she lets her head fall back against the door.

Her eyes flutter open, her blues on mine. She narrows them on mine, her tongue sticking out to wet her lips.

"I'm yours," she says. I smile down at her.

"Good girl." Then, I scoop her up and carry her to the bed. I tug down the comforter because I don't want her to worry about it, and let it fall to the floor. I lay her down gently, staring down at her. Her long locks taper out around her, her red sweater bunched up above the waistline of her jeans. "I am going to spend the next few hours letting you know how much every"—I pause to kiss her cheek—"single"—then her lips—"inch of you"—then her neck—"is loved."

Then, I get started. I reach down and unbutton and unzip her jeans, and she lifts her ass so I can tug them down. I drop them on the floor, my eyes dancing back up her legs to the soft, pink thong she has on. I reach up and tug her sweater off, letting her lie in front of me in just her bra and panties. My dick is throbbing, but I know it's going to be a minute. I have things to worship first.

I run my hands up her legs to her thighs, pushing them apart gently. I run my nose down the fabric of her panties and inhale her, my eyes rolling back in my head at her scent. I'm salivating now. I slip a finger underneath it, up and down her pussy. And when I pull it out, it's wet. I slide it into mouth and smile down at her.

"You're already ready for me, baby?" I ask. She bites

her lip and nods, one hand sliding up between her breasts, the other sliding down to her panty line. I hook my fingers into the straps and slowly pull them down her legs, tossing them onto the floor, too. I kiss the top of her foot, then her calf, up to her knee, then lay her leg back on the bed. I let my fingers dance up her skin until they're at her center, and then I start to rub her clit gently as I lower my mouth to her.

"Relax, baby," I tell her. "Let Daddy take care of you." Then, I start making love to her pussy with my mouth. I lick her up and down, slowly at first, letting her juices cover my tongue and spill out onto my beard. I kiss her, sucking her into my mouth, swirling my tongue around her lips while my finger continues to massage her, applying pressure with every circle. Then, I feel her body start to react the way she does before she comes undone. I slide one finger inside of her, then another, and start to move side to side as I suck her clit into my mouth. I pause for just a moment. "Let yourself go, sweet girl. Come for me. Let me taste all of you." She presses her head back into the mattress, one hand clawing at the sheets while the other presses my head deeper into her.

"Oh, Cash, I... Cash, I... Oh!" she cries out, her legs shaking and dropping to the sides while her body tenses, then releases into the bed. My hand is soaked, and so is my beard, and so is the bed. And I cannot wait to roll around in each other.

"That's my girl," I tell her just before I reach up and tug my own shirt off. She catches her breath and pushes herself up to sit as she reaches for my belt and undoes my pants.

"I want you in my mouth," she whispers, and I feel all the blood that's left in my body stream to my dick. Without hesitating, she yanks my pants down and pumps her hand up and down on my cock until it's standing at perfect attention. Then, she grabs my ass and pulls me into her, wrapping her lips around my tip and sucking me into her mouth. She moves her head back and forth and back and forth, and she swirls her tongue around my tip, and she takes me deep into her mouth. I clutch onto her hair as she moves. Then, as I feel myself about to hit the peak, I pull myself out of her mouth.

"Okay, baby," I tell her. I reach around and unclasp her bra, the last barrier between us falling to the ground. I bend down to my wallet in my jeans and grab a condom out of them. I tear it open while I look down at her, ready and waiting, pussy so wet it's glistening in the dim room light. It's so fucking sexy that her pleasuring me makes her wet. Almost as hard as I get by watching her writhe beneath my mouth. I grab hold of each of her thighs, then push myself into her, her whole body clenching around me as she takes me in. I feel her nails dig into my arms as she adjusts to me, and I clench my jaw and blow out a tight breath as I try not to blow my load before I even move.

But God, she makes it so hard.

Literally.

I start moving, slow at first, then faster, building up the momentum. She reaches up and pinches one of her nipples, rubbing and squeezing on her own tit until I think I'm gonna bust. I bend down and take the other into my mouth like I'm starving for it, and she moans my name. I swirl my tongue around her nipple, letting it slide between my teeth before I release it. I pull back, and she looks up at me.

"I want to ride you," she says with a devilish grin.

I pound into her again before I slide out.

"Yes, ma'am," I say as we quickly switch places. I lie back against the sheets as she crawls up me, straddling me so that she's positioned directly over me. She leans forward, licking my neck, then my bottom lip, before she sucks it into her mouth, tugging it gently with her teeth. Then, she pushes herself up, lowering her pussy down to my cock. But she doesn't take me inside her—not yet. Instead, she rides my shaft, back and forth, back and forth, dragging her wetness up and down it.

"You want this?" she asks. I lick my lips, my fingers digging into her hips.

"Right fucking now," I say.

She smiles as she continues moving back and forth, her folds sliding against me.

"Tell me."

I smile.

My girl likes it when Daddy tells her what to do—at least, in the bedroom.

"Take me inside of you, right now," I growl, "and ride me till I come inside of you."

She licks her lips, lifts her ass, then slides her pussy down, taking me inside of her in one, swift move. I press my head back, arching my back, bracing for it.

She starts rocking on me, slowly at first, then faster as she finds the rhythm that makes her whole body lose total control.

"That's it," she says as she moves faster and faster. "That's it right there."

That's all I need to hear. I grip her hips again, and this time, I take over. She found the spot, and now I'll take care of it. I move my hips up and down off the bed, knowing how close I am to coming, but knowing all the while that I will do my damndest to hold off until she does. I start to fuck her so hard and fast that she stops moving altogether, letting me take over. I feel her nails dig into my chest as her head drops back.

"Oh...I...oh," she says, and I see a tear of pleasure forming in her eyes. I'm streaming with sweat, and just as she goes rigid and collapses on top of me, I explode inside of her. We lie there for a moment, me still inside of her, both of us drenched in sweat, catching our breath. Finally, she rolls off me, and I roll over to kiss her neck, her shoulders. She curls up on top of my outstretched arm, and I kiss her hair, letting my fingers draw lines down her back. After a few more minutes, I slide off the bed, pulling her off after me. We walk to the bathroom, and I start the shower, letting the steam fill up the bathroom. I help her step in, and then I wash her from head to toe, trailing kisses over every inch of her as I go.

We finish up and climb back into the bed, and then she curls up against me again. And I breathe her in, watching as her breaths grow longer and shallower. She finally drifts, and I'm left to my favorite view. Just her and me, with nothing between us, and a lifetime in front of us.

And as she lies here, completely at peace, completely loved, I have this thought.

I think I might deserve this.

CHAPTER TWENTY-ONE

I HAVEN'T BEEN this nervous in a very, very long time.

I've been nervous to meet boyfriends' parents, family, grandmas.

But I've never had to meet a boyfriend's child.

A grown child, at that.

I'm chewing on my nail as he pulls up to the house and turns off the engine. He takes my hand in his and kisses it.

"Baby, you have to stop," he says with a smile. "She's not a snake. She's my daughter. And I think we're a lot alike. Which means she's going to love you."

I look at him and smile, blowing out a long breath.

"Come on," he says.

We walk up the front walk to the big, beautiful, brick Victorian in front of us, and Cash rings the doorbell. The door opens, and a beautiful woman with curly brown hair answers the door. She smiles so big when she sees us that it almost looks fake.

"Hi!" she cries before wrapping Cash in a long, shaky hug. Then, she does the same to me.

"Oh my gosh, you must be Stevie," she cries out once we come apart. "I'm Kaydee. It's so nice to meet you."

"So nice to meet *you!*" I say, and I mean it. In some ways, it would be weird to meet the love of my life's past love. God knows that was a slippery slope in my past life. But right now, I'm so excited to be here. I'm excited to get a glimpse into the young Cash. I'm excited to hear about their younger years. And I'm excited to watch Cash continue to see that he didn't ruin anyone's life. That he deserves his happiness because Kaydee got hers. Because Eden has had a good life. And now, he gets to be a part of it.

Rob comes around the corner from the kitchen, just as glowing as Kaydee, shaking our hands and introducing himself. And then I see her, like a princess being introduced into a ball. Not really—she has on ripped jeans and white Vans with a baggy sweater—but she's the most beautiful girl I've ever seen.

She has her mom's hair and long, lean figure, but when she smiles, she's all her dad. And how I love her already. She looks right at me, our eyes locking, and she makes her way across the foyer to me.

"I am so freakin' glad I am finally meeting you—for real, this time," she says, then to my surprise, she wraps her arms around me in a long, tight hug. When we come apart, she hugs Cash, and Kaydee ushers us all into the living room. Rob and Cash are talking about football and Rob's handiwork around the house. Kaydee and I chat about our jobs, Blue Bay, and the weather, but not in a boring, awkward, small-talk kind of way. She tells me about the weather in Boston and what I should be prepared for now that we've made the move. And that she and Rob would like to take us out to some of their favorite places around town once we settle in. Then, she sneaks off to the kitchen to take the food out, and I'm alone with Eden. My boyfriend's daughter.

The child of the love of my life.

"So," she says, taking a seat next to me on the couch, "were you afraid to meet me?"

I smile and shake my head.

"Afraid? No. A little intimidated, maybe," I say with a chuckle.

She smiles.

"That's fair. At least I'm not, like, twelve. Then, you'd have to worry about all the pre-teen hormones and shit."

I laugh again.

She's funny, like her dad.

"That's true. So, graphic design, huh?" I ask her. She smiles and nods.

"Yep. This is the part where you ask me what I'm gonna do with it when I graduate?" she asks with a smirk. I laugh again and shake my head.

"Nah. You seem like you have a good head on your shoulders. Besides, if anyone can tell you that *nothing* goes according to plan, it's me. Trust me. Just have fun with your life."

Her eyes widen, and she nods her head slowly.

"Wow. That's probably the best advice I've ever gotten. Thanks," she says. I nod and smile. There's a short silence, and I realize that both of our eyes have drifted across the room to him, standing there, one hand wrapped around his beer, the other in his pocket.

He's so goddamn beautiful.

"My mom was always afraid that if we found him too early, that I wouldn't get the 'best' of him. And I get it, ya know? After going through what she did, getting clean for me, I wouldn't want that around my kid. I wouldn't even want to take a chance with it," she says. I nod.

"Absolutely. I wouldn't either," I say.

"After we met with him a few months back, she smiled the whole drive home. She just kept crying, and when I'd ask her why, she said they were happy tears. Because he had found himself again. He was the version of him that she had always hoped I would get to have in my life." She turns to me, and I look at her. "I'm the only person in this room whose life he came into *after* you did. I can tell that you are a big part of the reason why he is this version—the best version, as my mom says. So, thank you. And thanks for being so cool about all of this."

I feel myself getting a little emotional as I look at her, a genuine smile on her face. She's so wise for twenty-two. Wiser than I ever was at that age.

"Thanks for letting me be a part of it, Eden," I tell

her. "I'm excited about this. All of this," I say, motioning to everyone in the room in their separate corners.

"Do you have any kids?" she asks. Then, she catches herself. "Ugh. Sorry. I hate when people ask personal questions like that. I just…I don't know. I feel like you would be a really good mom."

I smile and pat her hand.

"That means a lot coming from someone who obviously had the best," I say, nodding to Kaydee as she enters the room.

"I know I wasn't the easiest all the time," Eden says, standing up as Kaydee motions for all of us to come into the dining room. "And I know that I still have a lot of life to live and that it won't all be easy, either. I'm glad I found him."

My eyes drift back to Cash again, and this time, he's staring right back at me, that big, warm smile on his face.

"So am I."

Later that night, we're lying in bed. In *our* bed, in *our* house that we found together. We got ourselves a little Cape Cod style house about twenty minutes outside of the city, and we spend our weekends fixing it up, redecorating, and then re-redecorating when I change my mind. And I wouldn't have it any other way. And really, I don't think he would, either. My head is on his bare chest, and he's scratching the back of my head lightly.

"Seeing you two together today, smiling," he says, "I don't think I've ever been happier in all my life than seeing that."

I rest my chin on my hand and look up at him.

"I was pretty happy, too," I tell him. "She's a special woman. Thank you for letting me experience all of this."

He lifts my chin and kisses me softly.

"Are you kidding me?" he says. "Thank *you* for holding my hand and doing it with me. All of it. Eden, the move, the house. All of it. In a matter of months, you have changed my whole world. I wish I could explain to you what you have done for me, to me. I wish you could see you the way I do. How my every thought begins and ends with you. You're everything, Stevie. You have switched up my orbit, Stevie Sunshine. And I am so fucking grateful that you did."

He kisses me again, and I lay my head back down next to him, watching as his eyes slowly close as he drifts off into sleep, his hand still on my bare back. My eyes well with tears when I look at him. Because as much as I love this man, I know he loves me back, just the same. I know that I stop his world from turning. I know that his chest tightens a little bit each time we part. I know that he gets that same flutter that I do whenever he sees me walk into a room. I know that he gets that feeling of balance whenever we're near each other.

Sometimes, when we're together and he's sleeping like this, my mind drifts to Cade and Tess. How I cursed them at first. How, despite everything, they still wound up finding each other. And then, I realize that they were just a stepping stone for me to get to this point. This place, right here, with him.

The heartbreak, the betrayal, the loneliness. Everything was so that I could find this. Find him. Find someone whose days start and end with me, just like mine do with him. Just like the Earth finds the sun, I know that if we were to ever part, we'd find each other over and over again.

epilogue

cash

"ONE MORE," I say, opening my mouth wide for her to put another chip in. She laughs as she puts one in, then rolls the bag into a ball and puts it on the ground with the other snacks we've blown through on the drive.

It's been almost a year.

It's been one whole year since we made the move to Boston, and I can't believe how fast it's gone. She kept her same job, and I got a job at a contracting firm outside of Boston. Turns out, Marie used to work for them and still had some connections. Now, I'm a handyman, but I'm getting paid a little more for it.

We're still fixing up the house. Although, we're running out of projects. I'm sure she will find something else for us soon.

Eden graduated a few months ago and got this kick-ass job at this contracting firm outside the city—which happens to be the same one her dad works at. She's a junior graphic designer on their communications team, which means that I get to see my daughter at work every single day.

She has a new girlfriend who's a few years older but much less "bougie," so they seem happy. She shares an apartment with two other girls in Cambridge, and we do monthly dinners over at Kaydee and Rob's.

I don't know how I would have been as a dad. I don't know if I would have raised her right. Lord knows, I didn't have the best example. I still get sad that I missed out on so much. But my God, I'm so glad I get to be with her now.

She and Stevie have grown close and even meet for lunches together every few weeks in the city. It's a special thing to watch—one of the loves of your life with the other. There isn't anything in the world that makes me feel as whole as they do.

And right now, Stevie and I are about twenty minutes outside of Blue Bay to celebrate the year we've had. Marie's letting us use the cottage, and we have some of our favorite things planned—at least, she thinks we do. We stop at Mickey's, even though it's the evening, and get a cup of coffee and a hug for old time's sake. We grab a pretzel at Maude's, then some actual food, and head to the cottage.

We finish our burgers and our coffee, and then I light the fire while she curls up on the couch. We haven't been here in a year, but everything feels so much the same. I turn off the lights, so the only glow is from the fire. And then, I slide under the blanket next to her, and I let her drape her legs across mine. She takes a sip of the glass of wine she poured and sets it on the coffee table in front of us.

"Man," she sighs, "it feels surreal being back here."

I smile as I rub her leg.

"It really does," I tell her. "It feels like we blinked, and we were back."

I feel my heart rate picking up as I try to keep my calm.

I pat the bulge in my pocket for the fiftieth time, making sure the box didn't somehow fall out of my pants between the kitchen and here.

"But in some ways, it feels like it's been ages," she says. "So much has happened in the last year."

I nod and kiss her forehead.

"So much," I agree. Then, I look down at her. "Does it make you happy, baby? Are you happy with all that's happened?"

She looks up at me, her eye big and wide.

"I have never been happier," she says. Then, she spins around to look at me. "Do you know what you've given me? You gave me a love like I have never known. You gave me family that loves me. You gave me a shot at feeling like a mom. You have given me everything."

Okay, she's sort of stealing my thunder. I smile and clear my throat.

This is it.

I reach into my pocket and pull out the box.

"Well, Stevie Sunshine, you *are* everything." I slide off the couch onto my knee and look up at her. Her eyes drop from mine, to the box, and then bounce back up to mine. Her jaw drops, and I smile. "Let me keep you. Let me give you all that I have. Will you be my wife?"

I see her chest heave as she clasps her hand to it, the nails on her other hand digging into mine.

"Are you...are you sure?" she asks, covering her mouth now to stifle a smile. I laugh and nod my head, but I also want to take her in my arms and remind her how I can't be without her.

"Woman, don't you know that you're a part of my soul? I need you," I tell her. The tears well in her eyes, and she nods her head over and over again, sticking her hand out to me. I pull the diamond out of the box and push it onto her finger, kissing her hand, her wrist, her arm, and then taking her face in my hands and kissing her lips.

"Say it again," she whispers, a soft sob escaping her lips.

"I need you, Stevie," I tell her, kissing her again. "You are my heart"—I kiss her again—"my soul"—and again—"my sun. And I will never get sick of reminding you of that."

one year later

BONUS EPILOGUE

Want more of Stevie and Cash's story? **Sign up for my newsletter (bit.ly/uwts-bonus)** and get the bonus epilogue delivered right to your email or device!

night & day duet

BOOK TWO

Have you read Tess and Cade's story? Check out book one in the Night & Day duet, **Marks On the Moon.**

Still not done with this series? Try my spinoff novella, **Due North!**

about the author

T.D. Colbert is a romance and women's fiction author. When she's not chasing her kids or hanging with her husband, she's probably under her favorite blanket, either reading a book, or writing one. T.D. lives in Maryland, where she was born and raised. For more information, visit www.tdcolbert.com.

Follow T.D. on **TikTok, Instagram, and on Facebook, Author T.D. Colbert,** for information on upcoming books!

Are you a blogger or a reader who wants in on some secret stuff? Sign up for my newsletter, and join **TDC's VIPs** - T.D.'s reader group on Facebook for exclusive information on her next books, early cover reveals, give- aways, and more!

www.ingramcontent.com/pod-product-compliance
Lightning Source LLC
Chambersburg PA
CBHW060439180626
46817CB00007B/2890